TOE TO TOE WITH

A DRUNKEN

PHILOSOPHER

TOE TO TOE WITH A DRUNKEN PHILOSOPHER

Wondering in Small-Town America

Continuing the Dancing Deer Series

By Ron Lambert

Copyright © 2012 by Ron Lambert

Published in the United States by:

Printers Guild Publishing House, llc

425 Spring Street, Suite 101
Columbus, Texas 78934-2461
(979) 732-2962   Fax (979) 733-0015
www.printersguildpublishing.com

ISBN 978-0-9855083-7-1

Contents

PART I   **THE PHILOSOPHER**

PART II   THE PRIEST

PART III   THE GREAT DEBATE   205

Toe to Toe with a Drunken Philosopher is a work of Fiction

Except for some historical personages the names, characters, and incidents of the story are used fictitiously and do not represent any actual person or event.

Some of the towns, cities, or geographic localities are real. An interested reader might be able to find Lee Mountain, the Buffalo River, the Illinois Bayou, the Big Piney, Moccasin Gap, or even Little Creek's water crossing. Eudy's might be harder.

The author grew up in a small rural community and saw wonder in all living things. He wrote this story using the hazy remembrances of a child's fertile imagination and sheer luck.

Trademarks

Red Wing Shoes, *The Courier Democrat*, *The Kansas City Star*, *The Arkansas Gazette*, *The Memphis Globe*, *Grit*, Sears Roebuck and Co, Montgomery Ward, and all other trademarks are property of their respective owners. Printers Guild Publishing House, llc is not associated with any product or vendor mentioned in this book.

Cover

Art from Dreamstime.com

PART I
THE PHILOSOPHER

CHAPTER 1—FIRST DAY
Monday, September 6, 1943

"Take a seat." Heck Stout walked to the blackboard and wrote his name, the title of the course he taught, and the four rules he expected his students to live by. Rule number one was, *No talking*. Rule number two was, *No sleeping*. Rule number three was, *If you have something to say to the class, raise your hand for permission to talk*. And rule number four was, *If you absolutely have to talk, refer back to rule number one*.

To Heck, being a teacher was the fulfillment of a lifelong dream. He wanted to stand behind the lectern and spew forth bits of information archived from an earlier life. He wanted to say life was absurd, the world was chaotic, and each individual was at the mercy of an unforgiving and uncaring universe. He wanted to say that life was complicated, that it was up to the individual to make sense of his situation, and that each person—and each person alone—was responsible for his actions and his place in society.

When the bell rang telling the students they should be in their assigned classroom and for the teacher to commence instruction, the students still milled around the pencil sharpener and the desks of the more popular students.

Heck turned to his charges, then walked to the front of his desk. "Class, take a seat." From a stack of papers he selected the attendance sheet and started putting faces with the names called.

"This course is World History and is broken down into two semesters. In the first we'll study the beginning of civilization to the fall of Rome. When we return in January we'll review the material covered and close the first semester with finals.

"The second semester will begin with the Dark Ages, then we'll go through the Middle Ages and the Renaissance into the Age of Enlightenment and on to modern times. There will be major tests at the conclusion of each stage of civilization with the second semester finals during the penultimate week in May of next year.

"An essay of ten pages will be assigned each semester and pop quizzes will be sprung as I deem necessary. I do not give extra credit assignments. Whatever grade you make is the one you'll live with.

"Yes, sir. You on the back row with your hand up."

"Uh. Mister Stout, uh, which week is the penultimate one?" Laughter erupted.

"Calm down class." Heck looked intently at the student making the most noise of hilarity. "You, sir. You on the second row." A nervous young man pointed at his chest with a questioning look on his face. Heck locked eyes with the student and said, "Yes, you. Please tell the class which week is the penultimate one."

"I have no idea."

"Does anyone know? No? Well, it was a proper question and should have been asked." Heck looked at the student who had asked. "And your name?"

The young man stood beside his chair. "Baker, sir. Brad Baker."

"It's the next to last, Mr. Baker."

Johnston Baker's son sat down with red covering his face like a ripening tomato. Heck Stout picked up his lecture again with, "Let's have a look at our textbook. If you look at the copyright page you can see when the book was new. Our book was first published in 1930. That makes it thirteen years old. Now a book like this takes several years from conception to copyright. Does anyone think the author anticipated what would now be happening in Europe and North Africa from twenty years ago?

"When he wrote our book Hitler was in jail, Russia was run by the Bolsheviks led by Lenin, and here in the United States we were in the middle of the roaring twenties. The Charleston was the great rage and the Great War—the war touted to be the war to end all wars—had just ended. Do you think the author had any inclination a dictator named Stalin would lead Russia after the workers overthrew the Tzar with the Bolshevik Revolution? A second German military build-up? The Great Depression?

"No one has an opinion? I guess we can be thankful we're studying world history from the beginning because we are in tumultuous times and the last few chapters are in a state of flux. To help supplement our author's information I'd like for each of you to start reading the newspaper and listening to the world news on the radio. Tell your parents it's an assignment. Maybe they'll purchase you your own receiver so they won't miss their regular programs. Or you might tell them to listen with you, because those people who do not know history are doomed to repeat it."

When the bell rang its mechanized announcement, "You got five minutes to get to your next class," several were looking through their papers to see if world history was required for graduation.

Heck's second class was Beginning Philosophy. His daily schedule was two courses in world history and two courses in philosophy—one of each in the morning and then again in the afternoon. He also taught typing sandwiched in before lunch and again immediately after lunch. And an occasional assignment at cafeteria duty was thrown in for good measure.

At the blackboard Heck changed the title of his class to Beginning Philosophy and left the four rules. Low murmuring and snickering ruled his day. "Evidently," he thought, "these kids do not expect to actually learn anything. School's simply a location for honing social skills."

Heck had a difficult task. He was determined to give these young adults something to think about, to mold their minds with interesting information, to train them to think coherently, to teach them to express their thoughts in meaningful and complete sentences. Heck wanted to give them the means to rule the world.

That evening Heck and his wife sat at the dinner table with two children picking at their food. Otis was in third grade and May had just started first. Heck spent the previous seven years working in the Moccasin Gap sawmill for decent wages. But now, with both children in school and women joining the workforce to replace the men fighting the Axis forces, Janice Stout thought it was a good opportunity for her to get a job and let her husband quit his at the sawmill for a lower-paying one as a school teacher.

"Honey, tell me about your first day," said Janice as she brought a platter of sweet potatoes to the table. She continued with, "I've always heard the first day is the most important. It's when everyone finds out who's boss and what that boss will put up with."

"It's apparent the students are in charge and they're not gonna put up with much. I've decided that my lectures will have to be entertaining as well as informative. Tomorrow I'm going to start talking about mankind's beginning in the Euphrates valley in history, and the sophists and then, of course, Socrates himself in philosophy. If I can make it interesting enough I think I can put some cracks in their defensive armor. Right now they sit with their arms crossed daring me to teach them anything." Heck sprinkled hot pepper sauce on a huge helping of purple-hulled peas then said, "And how did your first day at the Livery Feed and Seed go? Did they have you currying horses?"

"I hope the bank calls soon. I had to mix the feed, water the stock, and fire up the stove for Mr. Jamison. He shoed horses all afternoon while I waited on customers. I caught my sleeve on fire at the stove and broke all my fingernails on his decrepit cash register."

Heck shook his head with lips pursed. "Janice, you didn't have to do this. I could have worked a few more years at the sawmill and probably made supervisor."

"I know, darling, but is that a proper job for someone like you? This teaching position is what you've always dreamed about. Well, not exactly high school. I think a job at the university is more in line with your credentials, but this is certainly a step in that direction." Janice glanced at the stove to make sure she had brought everything to the table. She then turned to the two children to see if they had actually added vegetables to their plates of meat. With both hands on her chair back she asked her two rambunctious children, "And did either of you have a good day?"

Otis had a mouthful of meatloaf so he nodded while May said her day had been great. She said she colored in the morning and listened to the teacher read a story in the afternoon. And recess had been best of all. She had ridden the merry-go-round while some irritating boy whirled it around trying to throw her off.

CHAPTER 2—SOCRATES
Tuesday, September 7,1943

"Socrates is known as the father of philosophy. At the time he lived and for many years after, philosophy was an umbrella term for wisdom, learning, intelligence, and various fields of study. Has anyone read anything by Socrates?"

Heck looked around the room. No hands showed. "Good. Because Socrates didn't write anything down. What we know of the man we get from people trailing along behind like puppies after a food bowl. They later reminisced over what they could remember him saying and wrote it down. His greatest pupil was Plato. I've heard that one important philosopher said, and I quote, '. . . the safest general characterization of the western philosophical tradition is that it consists of a series of footnotes to Plato.' . . . meaning the words of this great man is the source upon which everything philosophically known about our world is based. And he learned a great deal of what he knew from his master, Socrates.

"Mr. Runyon, would you nudge your friend. I fear we've lost him to Hypnos, the goddess of sleep. Mr. Mitchell, did you rest well last night?"

"Like a baby." Paul Mitchell stretched his lips in a cavernous yawn.

"Does that mean your mother brought you something to drink at four in the morning?" The class erupted in laughter. Paul Mitchell was the star basketball player and had been for the previous three years. The coaches at Skunk Hollow, the major adversary of Dancing Deer, thought Paul should have graduated by now. They thought Paul's coach must be making him take his senior year again just so Dancing Deer could prevail against their Skunk Hollow team one more time. Even Paul was worried. If he didn't pass so be it. He'd go through life almost finishing school. It wouldn't make any difference to him. He was going to raise cattle like his dad anyway. Why the hell did he need to know the Nile overflowed its banks every year depositing silt and making the land in

15

Egypt fertile, or why study philosophy in the first place? Why ask the big questions if no one knows the answers?

"Calm down, class. Let's continue. Now prior to Socrates there were other men of learning and there were people needing what these men could teach. Athens was the first democratic government. There were slaves doing the work, rich people accumulating assets, and poor people wanting to take what the rich people had. Just like today, if you have anything of value you have to keep it safe.

"In Athens a man could be charged with a crime against another and, if found guilty, he could lose his assets to the person he had wronged. So a man of means had to be constantly on the lookout for an opportunist seeking to rob him in court. Most of the pre-socratic philosophers migrated from Miletus to Athens where, for a fee, they would instruct the sons of the wealthy in the intricacies of swaying public opinion in their favor. They knew the art of rhetoric, or of stating a series of facts in such a way as to deduce a truth in their favor. These men were called sophists and were hated by the majority of the citizens of Athens. Then, as now, only a few individuals were considered wealthy with the majority of the citizens less wealthy and trying to relieve their neighbors of that wealth. The practice of charging fees for their teaching prompted Plato to call the sophists '. . . shopkeepers with spiritual wares.'

"Two prominent sophists were Protagoras and Gorgias. While Protagoras said that everything is true relative to the spectator, Gorgias denied there was any truth at all. He explained his reasoning by stating that one, nothing exists. Two, if anything did exist it was incomprehensible. And three, even if it might be comprehensible it could not be communicated."

"I see a bunch of blank faces. How many of you have read Chapter Two on the sophists?

Okay. there is no way you're going to understand this if you don't keep up with your assigned reading. Philosophy is a deep subject. Some of the greatest minds the world has produced have spent their lifetimes contemplating, pondering, and recovering from deep within their reasoning what you are free to read. Don't take this course lightly. It will help you through life's journey. I can help, but you have to meet me halfway. And if you do, you'll thank me—and these great thinkers—many years from now when you draw on them for guidance."

A hand shot up. "Isn't that what our religious faith supplies?"

"The philosophers we have studied so far lived in Greece and the surrounding city-states five hundred years before Christianity. The Islamic religion came along eight hundred years after Christ. So these Greeks had their own polytheistic religion prior to Christianity and well before Islam to contend with and one of the charges leveled against Socrates was impiety—or irreverence to those gods. Aristotle later faced this same charge.

"After Rome was sacked and barbarity ruled, the Greek philosophical texts were lost to the west. It was during these years that the authority of the church ascended in power to become the most influential institution in the western world. Only the Arabs kept the works of these great men available for study in translations to their own languages. Four hundred years later, ancient texts by Plato were uncovered in Rome and in the following centuries his works periodically appeared, translated from the ancient Greek—a language many western scholars had lost the ability to read—into Latin. Then in the middle ages, the thirteenth or fourteenth century, translated works of Aristotle were uncovered in Toledo in the possession of the Moors. Many Christian theologians spent their lives reconciling these newly re-discovered texts to Christianity. Their efforts were called Scholasticism. The most notable were from Saint Augustine, Anselm the Archbishop of Canterbury, and Boethius for Plato and Saint Aquinas for Aristotle. So, as you can see, what we are studying today was instrumental in establishing the morals and ethics that became associated with our religious beliefs. And they also helped provide the wisdom and the rationality we use today to make our day-to-day decisions."

Heck looked around his classroom and saw a sea of blank faces. "In Greece someone once asked Thales, if he was so smart why was he also so poor. That spring this philosopher noticed the rainfall was plentiful and spread out evenly over the growing season. He sold everything he owned and used his money to rent all of the olive presses for use later in the year. When the olives were harvested the olive-growers had to make arrangements with the philosopher to sub-lease his rented presses before they lost their pickings to spoilage. The philosopher became a very rich man. One story says that he gave his windfall profits to the poor, as money was not what gave him pleasure. He only wanted to make a point to his naysayers."

Paul poked Sarah Bingham through the rungs of her chair back and whispered, "Sarah, do you understand this crap?"

"Not all of it. Somebody needs to tell Mr. Stout we have other subjects to study. He only gets a part of our time."

"Coach says he's going to get me a tutor. He looked through my book and said it was all crap. None of this stuff has changed since the dinosaurs."

When the bell rang Paul Mitchell followed Sarah into the hall. "You think maybe you could help me get my assignments done?"

"Paul, I'm flattered you think I'm smart enough to help you, but I'm as lost as you. But, my mom knows this stuff. I'll get her to help me and then I'll help you. In the meantime you should read those chapters."

"Naw. I ain't got time. I just want to copy your homework and get the answers to the tests from over your shoulder. You want to get a soda at Eudy's after school?"

"Sure, that sounds swell."

CHAPTER 3—SARAH
Tuesday, September 7, 1943

"Inez, Inez, wait up. I'm carrying so many books I can't catch up."

"Here, give me your clipboard. Why have you got so many books, Sarah?"

"I've been talking to Paul and didn't have time to go to the locker."

Inez stopped. "Paul? Tall Paul?"

"Certainly. We're going to Eudy's after school."

"Tall Paul is taking you to Eudy's?"

"Inez, your mouth is hanging open. We're going to meet there. His coach told him he could miss practice while he lines up help for his classes. I'm going to help him with philosophy. Stout's being ridiculous with his assignments. He's given us a chapter in our book to read each night and wants us to discuss the main points each day in class."

"Whew. That's what I've heard. He stands in front of the class and lectures. Sometimes he asks the students questions or their opinions. He doesn't want facts, he wants their interpretations and impressions. I'm glad I'm not in there."

"I know. Isn't that the most obscene thing you can think of? I mean I might be able to memorize a date or a man's name but to give a few words on what he believes or how he knows something—why, that's just hateful."

"Sarah, tell me about Tall Paul. How'd he ask you? Is it a date? You going to date Tall Paul?"

"I might."

That night Sarah asked her mother if she knew anything about the philosophers before Socrates. "A little. I'm sure glad you're taking this philosophy course, honey. I had the best time when I took it. I hadn't met your father at that time and I thought my teacher was the smartest man alive. And all that smart was packaged in a rather nice box. Of course I wouldn't tell your father, but before I met him my philosophy teacher was my prince."

"Mom, that's just sick."

"Why do you think so? Is there not someone you'd like to be with when you close your eyes?"

"Uh, yeah, but not some overweight egghead. I think about boys my own age."

"I did as well, but most of them were—well, they were immature. I think girls develop into adults faster than boys. When I was in school most of the boys were interested in games that could help them determine where they stood in the pecking order. Besides physical strength there were other factors that came into play. Who could play the stupidest prank. Who could get away with the most outrageous behavior. Who could pass a course with the least amount of effort. Who could date the prettiest girl—who would cease to be the prettiest girl once she had been kissed or manhandled in some way. I wasn't interested in someone so childish as to see if he could sneak a snake into another person's locker or wanted someone else to do his homework, so the boy asking could while away his time cuddling up with some other girl."

"Mom, was that you before you met Dad?" Sarah pulled out a chair from the dining table and plopped down. She rested her head in two up-turned hands and, with a dreamy look on her face, asked, "Did some nice-looking boy ask you to help him with his homework?"

"No, honey, my best friend did a beautiful diorama for her biology class and a boy talked her into giving it to him so he could put his name on it and pull up a failing grade. My friend thought she had enough time to make a second, but she didn't."

"Why did she do it?" asked Sarah.

"Because he was popular and she thought he liked her."

"But he didn't?"

"No. He was just using her to get what he wanted. A common scenario. It still happens today even with adult men. I guess some of them never grow out of that infantile mindset. He promised to take her to a movie, but after she gave him the project he went his merry little way holding on to a girl who couldn't talk clearly for the wad of Double Bubble in her mouth."

"Boys are so juvenile. Dad wasn't that way was he?"

"He came along a little later. First was this teacher who spoke so eloquent, who said things that made me think, who seemed to be a man who could lull you into dreamland holding out his hand to guide your way. I was completely spell-bound.

"Then I met your father and he was everything I was looking for. He was closer to my own age, smart enough to participate in meaningful conversation, funny enough to keep me from being bored, and serious enough to plan for the future. He was also one handsome devil. And to top it all off he was a man of high ethical standards. You certainly wouldn't find him asking someone else to do his work."

"Do you think he'll be coming home soon?"

"I sure hope so, honey. According to his letters we're winning all the major battles. He and his buddies are chasing the Germans all the way back to Berlin. It's just a matter of time. My only hope is that he doesn't become so complacent that he gets reckless. Or so confident in his abilities that he gets shot trying to accomplish an impossible goal."

"Mom, I'm going to write Dad a letter."

"He'd like that, dear."

CHAPTER 4—THE SOPHISTS
Wednesday, September 8, 1943

"I assume everyone has read Chapter Two. So now put your books under your desks and take out a clean sheet of paper. We're going to have our first quiz." Heck walked to the blackboard and wrote two sentences, *(1) Name three philosophers who were sophists. (2) Give a famous quote attributed to each.*

Heck looked out over his pupils. No one was writing anything down. They stared straight at the blackboard like they couldn't believe what they were reading. One girl in the middle of the room tried to make eye contact. Heck wondered what was the matter. She jerked her head up, arched her eyebrows, and rolled her eyes. She was trying to tell him something.

"Okay, class, those are the questions for the first, third, and fifth rows. If you are seated on the second or fourth row, here are your two questions."

Heck walked to the right panel of the front blackboard and slowly picked up a piece of chalk. He thought for a moment and then wrote beside numeral one, *What was Plato trying to explain with the analogy of the cave?* And beside numeral two he wrote, *Why did Socrates not escape when given the opportunity?*

Heck spent the next ten minutes walking around the room observing the progress made by his students. Several people twirled their pencils. One boy tapped his fingers against the top of his desk. Others simply stared into space. Occasionally he heard low muffled voices and, like a boxer on a hurt opponent, he was there determining which student was talking. In ten minutes he told everyone to put their names at the top of the page along with the words, Philosophy, Morning Class. After retrieving the papers he said, "All right, class, open your books and use them to properly answer the questions on a clean sheet of paper. Remember rows one, three, and five answer the questions on the left board and rows two and four the right board. Two thirds of your grade will be based on the quiz and one third on the open book answers. Okay, class, let's get started. You have the rest of the class period."

While the class had their heads down and thumbing through their textbook Heck looked through the retrieved papers. From the thirty papers turned in, twelve were blank. He made a list of the students in attendance but without names on the papers turned in. With the twelve blank sheets he walked around the room and asked each student on his list to pick out his paper and to add his name to it.

The first boy said, "But, Mr. Stout, how am I supposed to know? There isn't anything written on any of these sheets of paper."

"That's right. I received twelve papers completely blank. And, of the eighteen with something written, none had your name. So pick one of the twelve that could have been yours and add your name to it. I need something to put an 'F' on."

Paul piped up from the desk behind the girl who had rolled her eyes. "This isn't fair. How were we supposed to know you were going to give a test."

"Yeah, this is only our third day in school. Most of us haven't bought pencils yet."

"And, Mr. Whittaker, how do you propose going through life never being ready? I told everyone the first day there would be pop quizzes. And I assigned the first two chapters. Yesterday I told you again to read your assignments, which now includes chapter three.

"Now, for twelve of you, it will take an 'A' on the next quiz to bring your average up to a 'C.' I suggest you take me seriously. What's more, those with failing grades will not be able to participate in any extracurricular event. That means no sports for the boys and no pep club for the girls. I think each one of you needs to prioritize what's important."

After fifteen minutes of profound silence the bell rang. Heck stood beside the classroom door and said, "Put your names on your answer sheets and give them to me as you leave the room. That'll be all class. See you tomorrow."

"Sarah, wait up. Yo, Sarah, you mad at me for not showing up yesterday at Eudy's?"

"No. I figured something came up. I only waited a few minutes."

Tall Paul took Sarah by the arm and said, "Let's go this way. My locker's down here."

"I can't. My locker is this way and I have to get to my next class in the gym. I don't have time."

"Can I see you after school? I really would like some help in philosophy. Coach said he'd pay for tutoring."

"A few of us are meeting in one of the study rooms in the library during lunch. You're welcome to join us."

"Instead of eating?"

"Yeah, I know. It's a hard decision. But, like Mr. Stout said, you have to prioritize."

"I can prioritize. I just can't go without eating."

"Then I'd suggest you actually read the assignments."

"Yeah, well, I think you're upset because I didn't show."

"Mr. Mitchell, I could care less what you think." Sarah then turned and started walking toward her locker.

Brad Baker was walking in front carrying so many books his clipboard fell and he stopped to pick it up. Sarah stopped behind him and waited. Brad straightened and said, "What do you think of philosophy?"

"I think it's a fascinating class. I've been wondering how I've gotten this far and not heard any of this stuff before."

"You mean you're not dropping the class?"

"Good heavens, no. This is the most interesting class I've got. However, it also might be the one requiring the most effort."

"I know. But I—you sure you're not going to change to Arkansas history or something?"

"No. I am not. This is just a challenge. I plan on leaving this class with something I didn't have when I came in." Sarah stopped at her locker and started twirling the locker knob while Brad continued down the hall wondering if he might stay another day or two before transferring.

CHAPTER 5—FAILING
Wednesday afternoon, September 8, 1943

"Paul, come in here for a minute." Coach John Jolly closed the office door behind his star center. "You doing all right in your classes?"

"No, sir. I'm having a hard time in world history and philosophy."

"That's what I was worried about. Do you think I should have a talk with Mr. Stout?"

"No, sir. I think I need to prioritize. I finally found my book and I plan on reading the first three chapters tonight. Today we had a pop quiz and I turned in a blank sheet of paper."

"Has Stout got it in for you? Has he singled you out for anything?"

"No, sir. Mr. Stout's a good teacher, I just don't understand what he's saying. He expects a lot out of us, not like some of the other teachers. Have you located me a tutor?"

"For world history. I don't know a soul who's ever taken anything in philosophy. I'll keep looking. Why don't you consider transferring to another subject? It's still early and I can get you a tutor for any of the other courses."

"I'll let you know after I've read these chapters. By the way, Sarah Bingham said her mother knows philosophy." Paul took the towel from around his neck and wiped the sweat from his forehead. "Do you know when Mr. Stout will be informing the principal which students are failing?"

"I think you got a month. He'll have to give a test or two before he'll have any clear indication." Coach Jolly raised one leg resting a large cowboy boot on a stack of uneven papers. "That's enough to get us through the Scranton and Pottsville games. I don't know about the homecoming game against Skunk Hollow. That might be pushing our luck a bit.

"In the meantime I'll keep looking for a tutor. I've already lined one up for world history. Paul Nelson has agreed to help us out on

Tuesday and Thursday evenings between six and eight. I'll give you his address tomorrow. You're scheduled to start next week. We don't have any games scheduled for the weekends so it looks like the tutor for philosophy will have to meet with you sometime Saturday. Will that be all right with you?"

"Sure. Will you contact Mrs. Bingham?"

Jolly raised his second leg. He now had both cowboy boots on his desk, one on top of the other. His seatback leaned at a precipitous angle, "Yeah. I'm glad you found her. She's the only candidate I've got. But be sure and mind your manners. I don't think there's a man about, as her husband is fighting in Europe. We certainly don't want to get any rumors started."

"I don't mind meeting with her in the library or one of the classrooms."

The coach thought for a moment, then said, "I'll let her know." John Jolly looked at his empty trophy case. "Paul, you could take social studies and this would be so much easier."

"Listen, Mr. Jolly, could I cut out early? I got to read those three chapters tonight."

"Yeah, sure. But you be here all that much earlier tomorrow afternoon. We got to get the pitch and run from the post going."

"Coach, did you know that they offered to let Socrates escape? They even had him a boat tied to the dock. His jailer said he could leave, turned his back, and walked into another room. Socrates wouldn't have any of it. He stayed."

"Stayed for what?"

"Socrates, Mr. Jolly. I'm talking about Socrates."

"Who the hell is Socrates?"

"Socrates. The person the Delphic Oracle Priestess said was the smartest man in the world."

"The Delphic what?"

CHAPTER 6—TALL PAUL
Wednesday evening, September 8, 1943

"Son, what book you reading?" Paul's mother noticed Paul had been reading a heavy book since he finished supper.

"It's a book on philosophy. These men in Greece tried to figure out how things work. Well, not things exactly, but how we work. How we fashion ideas, how we reason, form conclusions, solve puzzles, and grow in wisdom."

Paul's dad lowered the *Marsden County Meteor* and said, "Did those men not have to work?"

"That's also interesting. This takes place in Athens, Greece, where the people lived in a democratic society. Most people owned slaves who did the work so the men spent their time dressed in sheets and talking about things they dreamed up. Each one tried to live his life in some meaningful way that was different from anybody else's. Here's a picture of one man who lived in a burial pot." Paul took his book to his father and pointed to a picture of Diogenes sitting in a large clay bowl turned on its side.

"Son, how will knowing this stuff make you a smarter man?"

"I don't know. But the smartest man I know is teaching the class. If he got that way from reading books like this, then I haven't got anything to lose but a portion of my time and the possibility of gaining a lot."

"Son, I think you're getting smarter already. I'm all for it if it's not going to interfere with your chores or shooting hoops."

"Frank, let the boy read the book. I'm excited for him. Life must have more meaning than bringing in eggs or milking the cow. This philosophy sounds like it might be something I'd be interested in. Are there any love interests?"

"No, Mom. I don't think there are many female philosophers. However, I have glanced through the book and there are some romances talked about. Soren Kierkegaard, a deeply religious man from Denmark, loved a woman dearly and even proposed marriage before he got cold feet."

"He reneged?"

"Yep. Said he had to devote all his time figuring things out and thought marriage would be a distraction."

Paul's mother took a dishtowel and wiped dry a small bowl. "Son, you ought to burn that book. There's a woman involved in that story who won't have grandchildren to spoil."

CHAPTER 7—A MEETING OF THE MINDS
Monday, September 13, 1943

"Amos, I got to have Tall Paul or we're gonna lose most of our games."

"You've got an entire school, half of them boys. Why would one young man make such a difference?"

"Because that one young man is six foot seven and as agile as a cat. If I can't have him, then the best I can do is like all the other years we've had. For every two we win we lose three."

Amos Considine was the school principal. He closed a sheaf of papers and placed them in an open briefcase. "He's been the star on your team since he was a freshman and we haven't had a winning year yet."

Coach Jolly glanced over his boss's desk to see if the latest edition of the town's newspaper might be handy. "I know. But this year's different. He's all we had in those years and this year we've got a few other players who have improved their skills enough to help."

"I thought you said without him it would be like all the previous years."

"I did. It was only through providence and my good coaching that we won a few games. Without him the rest of the boys won't have an anchor. And, as good a coach as I am, I don't think I can get the remaining team to play to the best of their abilities when we have our best player sitting in the bleachers."

"John, here's what you do. You get that boy some help. I'll slide you some money to pay for a tutor and you make sure he has time to do his studies. If he's that good an athlete, then he's probably also smart enough to make a passing grade. I'm not asking for honor roll grades just something passing in all his courses."

"Amos. He ain't smart. The kid's as dumb as a post. I'm not sure he knows how to read or write. But you should read what they said about his ball-playing in last Saturday's paper."

"Then how did he make it to his senior year?"

31

"I think most of his teachers have been sports enthusiasts."

"Damnit, John, if he don't make the grade he ain't going to play. I don't care if he's eight feet tall. You get him a tutor and get his grades up or you can have another losing season and look for another job next summer."

"Okay. Okay. He's passing—just barely—everything except World History under Heck Stout and Beginning Philosophy, again taught by Stout. I've lined up someone to help him with world history, but so far I haven't found anyone for that crap course in philosophy. I think Stout has it in for him. Maybe you could talk to the man. Make sure it's nothing personal. Let him know we need the kid. Hell, Stout's probably an atheist anyway."

"Mr. Jolly, I don't mix politics and religion here. I suggest you find a way to solve your problems without pushing off the blame to someone else. Now get to it."

John Jolly left the principal's office under a cloud of despair. It was time to talk to Mrs. Bingham.

"Hello, Mrs. Bingham?

"No. This is Sarah. I'll get her. May I tell her who's calling?"

"Yeah, Sarah. This is Coach Jolly"

In a few minutes a lower and more expressive voice came on the phone. "Mr. Jolly, I'm Sarah's mother. What can I do for you?"

"Mrs. Bingham, I understand you are knowledgeable in the field of philosophy. If that's true, the high school would like to hire you to tutor a student."

"One student?"

"Yes. He's a very important student. He's Tall Paul, our starting center in basketball."

"I see. And he can't play if he has bad grades?"

"Mrs. Bingham, you've hit the nail on its head with the first swing."

"And this Tall Paul, does he want to learn philosophy or does he simply want to play basketball?"

"Ma'am, I'd rather you talk to him and make up your own mind. He's a real nice kid but not so bright."

"Mr. Jolly, I'll think about it and let you know."

"Wait, Mrs. Bingham. There isn't anyone else who can do it. You have to accept. As a way of thanking you, I can give you and Sarah free tickets to all of the basketball games this fall and baseball games in the spring." Coach Jolly paused a moment before he continued. "And if you don't help the boy his dreams of playing professional will flit out the window. What with his mother sick and him managing the farm by himself I can understand why he falls asleep after reading a few pages."

"All right, Mr. Jolly, but I want to talk with him first."

"Saturday morning at ten convenient for you?"

"Yes, I guess so. Be sure and tell him to bring his book."

"I will. Thank you, Mrs. Bingham. You have made my day."

CHAPTER 8—MRS. BINGHAM
Saturday, September 18, 1943

"Mom, Paul is our star basketball player. He scored thirty-five of our fifty points against Scranton last night. It was the first game of the year and the first time we've won the first game of the year since, since probably ever. Everyone in school is ecstatic. We're thinking we may have a winning season this year. Of course, if Paul doesn't play we don't have a chance. I think Coach Jolly is banking on you to help Paul stay in the game."

"He still has to study. I can only help him if he does his part. Have you had any other tests besides that one pop quiz?"

Sarah was looking through her purse for lipstick. Not finding any, she wondered where she might have put it. Paul would be there any minute and she didn't want to look like plain vanilla. "No, that's been the only one so far. Also, we've been assigned a ten-page essay. I have to write about the Stoics."

A knock at the door. "I'll get it, honey. I'm sure it's the man of the hour." Regina Bingham walked to the front door and opened to a very tall and handsome young man. She held out her hand. "I'm Mrs. Bingham."

"Good morning, ma'am. I'm Paul Mitchell, the basketball player over his head in philosophy."

"Come on in. It can't be all that bad. Philosophy is an interesting field. You just can't treat it as a bunch of facts, but as a way of looking at things. Let's go into the kitchen so we can spread your materials out. Before we get started would you like a cup of tea?"

"No, thank you, ma'am." Paul pulled out a chair and plopped down. He took a pencil from his shirt pocket and wrote the date on a blank page in his notebook.

"May I see your textbook?" Regina turned to the table of contents. After thumbing through the first few pages she sat the book down and asked, "What do you need help with, Paul?"

"All of it, Mrs. Bingham. I don't understand the forms of Plato, the universals of Aristotle, the Doctrine of the Mean, or why we don't live our lives like the Epicureans. It looks to me like doing the things that give us pleasure and not doing the things that bring us pain is the way to go as long as we don't inflict hurt on someone else."

For the next hour Regina gave him her basic perception to the field of study known as philosophy. Paul listened, asked questions, wrote notes, nodded his head, shrugged his shoulders, and pondered her questions. Sarah pulled up a chair into the hall where Paul couldn't see her and close enough that she could hear his answers to her mother's questions. When the hour was almost over she quietly picked up the chair and carried it into her bedroom. Then she walked into the living room, opened her own book, and started reading.

When Paul was being ushered to the front door he stopped and said, "Hello, Sarah. You come to the game last night?"

"No, but I understand you were the star and the only reason we won. How does it feel to be a hero?"

"Okay, but I'd rather someone thought I was smart. A person's athletic ability is only good for a few years, but his intelligence stays with him throughout his life."

Sarah didn't know what to say. After a moment Paul turned and walked to the door. Sarah said, "Hey, listen, you are Paul Mitchell aren't you? Not some imposter he's hired to take his place in class."

"Ha. That just means you don't know the real me. See you in school Monday." He turned to Sarah's mother. "Thank you, ma'am. I appreciate your help."

CHAPTER 9—HECK GOES TO CHURCH
Saturday, October 2, 1943

"Honey, tomorrow is your birthday. I was wondering if there was any particular thing I could do for you to make it a special day. Would you like for me to cook you breakfast and bring it to you in bed? Would you like to go to a movie? How about a soda at Eudy's?"

"Heck, would you go to church with me?"

"Church? You know how I feel about that."

"Yes, I know, but I also know that you love me and will do anything I ask if I ask the right way and at the right time. So tomorrow is my birthday and I want you to put on your best clothes and go to church and then I thought we'd eat at the new restaurant in town—the Bistro at the Ritz Grand Hotel and Ballroom."

Heck adjusted his glasses. "I'd rather pull out a fingernail, but it's your day. Whatever you want is what's gonna be."

The next morning Heck, Janice, Otis, and May walked the few blocks to the First Baptist Church. Heck took off his hat when entering the sanctuary and stood to one side as his family slid into a pew three quarters of the way toward the back. Heck sat next to the aisle. If he crossed his leg, his shoe would extend into an open area to the right of the pew in front. Several of Janice's friends came by and chatted while the sanctuary filled.

At exactly eleven o'clock a piano started playing and everyone still standing scrambled for a seat. For the next hour Heck listened to an educated man give a lecture on how people should live their lives according to the tenets of Christianity. The speaker then enumerated the advantages his flock would receive if they expressed their belief in Christ as the Savior for humanity. To Heck the main difference between theology and philosophy was that, according to most religions, you gave up the pleasures in this life to receive a life without toil and to be in the presence of the deity in the next. Being a modern philosopher, Heck thought there was no next life and that a person should live his life like this was it. Heck had to be careful. He was better off not telling his ideas to anyone. Especially if those thoughts were tossed in the air and came back to earth sifted by angels. Where an atheist or an agnostic does not care what his neighbor believes, most deeply religious people won't tolerate the companionship of an unbeliever.

Heck knew that sometime in the following week, but probably not Wednesday night, the Baptist minister and one or two others he brought for encouragement, would appear on Heck's doorstep to pressure him and the two children to join Janice into their fold of believers.

When leaving the church, the minister lurked at the exit of the sanctuary stopping people to shake their hands, to ask after their health, to receive praise for his insightful sermon, and to setup possible meetings in the upcoming week. When Heck and his family reached the spot the minister had staked out, the minister held out his hand. "Mr. Stout, I'm so glad to see you. My daughter says you're the best preacher teaching any of her classes."

"Preacher?"

"Yes, I know, but those were her exact words. She asked me to explain how Saint Augustine reconciled Plato's ideas with his religious beliefs. She said you called it Scholasticism. I've been spending as much time finding the answers to her questions as I have in preparing my sermons."

"I'm glad she's taking the course seriously. Philosophy does not have all the answers. Although it drives down lots of different avenues, philosophy doesn't profess to know even the right road to travel. It just opens a person's eyes and helps them determine what questions to ask."

"Mr. Stout, that will be next week's sermon. You and I need to spend some time together to discuss it in more detail."

Heck and the minister shook hands, then Heck and his family continued through the church vestibule toward the front door, letting the traffic jam that had piled up behind dissipate.

At the restaurant, Heck pulled out a chair for his adoring wife. Their table, covered in a white linen tablecloth and laden with neatly folded napkins and precisely planted tableware, awaited. The waiter said they could order from the menu or participate in the Sunday Brunch Buffet. It was all you could eat from several serving stations, and the children were charged half price. Later in the meal Heck was proud his children behaved, he had not made a remark decimating his stature as one of the city's more astute citizens, and he had been able to make his wife bubbling-over happy. Heck then noticed Otis loading his knife with english peas and letting them roll down the knife blade single file into the commodious expanse of an adolescent mouth. May had taken her spoon to make a lake of brown gravy inside her mashed potatoes. She was now positioning small pieces of carrots and bits of celery like opposing ships at sea. Heck looked at his wife. She was dabbing her eyes with a wadded up handkerchief.

CHAPTER 10—PREPARING FOR THE GAME
Tuesday, October19, 1943

"Good morning, class. Take your seats. We've got a lot of ground to cover today." Heck walked behind his desk and picked up a piece of chalk. On the blackboard he wrote, '*Compare Idealism with empiricism.*'

The students put their books under their desks and started writing furiously on blank sheets of paper. Heck sat down and began looking over his lecture outline. Today he planned on discussing Immanuel Kant, who claimed to have discovered the universal principles of thought that applied to the whole of humanity for all time.

After ten minutes Heck asked for the papers to be passed to the front, where Brad Baker stacked them together and placed them on a corner of Heck's desk.

"Today we're going to discuss Immanuel Kant, one of the most important philosophers to give us his perceptions from the time of Aristotle five centuries before the birth of Christ to Friedrich Nietzsche who died in 1900. Nietzsche is known for a remark attributed to him but actually taken out of context. The remark is, 'God is dead.'

"But back to Kant. He was a methodical bachelor who never veered far from his birthplace of Konigsberg in East Prussia. It was said that he was so regular in his habits that the women would set their clocks according to his daily walk past their houses.

"When he came into prominence the leading philosophers were at a stalemate. The rationalists claimed that metaphysical judgments— the fundamental principles upon which all knowledge is based—were known and justified purely by the intellect. The empiricists, in contrast, claimed the human mind was like a blank sheet of paper waiting to be written on by the world of experience."

Heck looked out over his class. All the chairs were full and the students were writing down everything he said. Lately when he lectured he had them sitting on the edges of their seats. This is what he lived for.

"Kant found a way to synthesize these two opposing views. He said that the mind acquires knowledge from experience and further argued that the mind imposes principles upon experience to generate knowledge."

Heck went to the blackboard, erased the question for the pop quiz, and wrote Kant's twelve fundamental judgments he called The Categories. When he finished writing the last one the bell rang and the class let out a large gasp of air. They gathered their books and waited for a second bell so they could storm through the door heading to their next class.

"Tomorrow I want the outlines to your ten-page essays. Also I want a brief synopsis and a list of your sources. The paper is due in three weeks. That's all, class."

Outside, Brad pushed his way through the mass of students until he walked beside Sarah, "What were you assigned to write about, Sarah? I got the Epicureans. Sarah?"

"What? Oh, I'm sorry, Brad, I was deep in thought. What did you say?"

"I asked if you had a date for the Homecoming Dance."

"No. I was planning on working on my paper. For some reason I can't get started. My mom says I am the world's worst procrastinator."

"If you would rather dress up and listen to a live band, to shuck your shoes, and slip and slide over a floor greased with cornmeal while I try to keep us balanced, then I would certainly jump at the opportunity to escort you."

"That's sweet, Brad. How long did you spend composing your request?"

"Most of last night."

"Thank you for asking, Brad. I'll let you know tomorrow."

Paul had been trying to catch up with Sarah to ask her to the homecoming dance. He was only two strides behind Brad when he heard Brad ask Sarah to the dance. She put him off. Now Paul had a decision to make.

When it was time for basketball practice, Paul went into Coach Jolly's office and left a note saying he couldn't practice because he had a heavy assignment in philosophy to work on.

When Coach Jolly arrived to start practicing his team he found the note and threw a satchel of papers across the room. Jolly stormed out looking for Heck Stout.

After checking Stout's empty classroom, Jolly went to the cafeteria, then to the library. He walked past the principal's office where he looked through the glass window beside the office door. Jolly had already decided that when he found Stout he would pop him one on the kisser. There had to be some rules. No teacher was going to interfere with his first winning season. So far Dancing Deer had won two games and the team was getting better all the time.

The building's front doors were propped open to allow the students an easy exit from the building. After leaving the principal's office, Coach Jolly noticed long lines of students waiting for their buses. Jolly went outside and saw Heck Stout keeping order in one of the lines. Coach Jolly stomped down the line of students and grabbed Stout by the shoulder. He spun the philosophy teacher around and slammed his fist into the side of Heck's face. Heck tumbled into a line of confused students.

Towering over the prone Heck, Coach Jolly pointed his finger and shouted, "You frigging atheist, leave my boys alone."

CHAPTER 11—IN THE PRINCIPAL'S OFFICE
Tuesday afternoon, October 19, 1943

Heck got to his feet, but Coach Jolly had already stormed off. What had gotten into him? What was he talking about leaving his boys alone?

One of the other teachers came over and gave Heck a dirty handkerchief. "Here, wipe that bloody nose on this. Uh, oh. Here comes the boss. Did you do anything to deserve this?"

"Mr. Stout, please come to my office. Someone else will make sure your students get on their buses."

Heck gathered himself and dutifully followed the principal through the crowd of students and teachers who had gathered in a circle to find out what happened. Scarcely had Heck gotten to his feet before the students who heard Coach Jolly's comments started telling the ones too far away what transpired. In the principal's office a secretary brought Heck a hand towel she had drenched in cold water before squeezing out the excess.

"Mr. Stout, what the heck happened out there?"

"I'm not sure. I was helping the kids from junior high get on their buses when Coach Jolly walked up from behind, jerked me around, and slugged me in the face. He then pointed his finger at me and said for me to leave his boys alone."

"What did he mean by that?"

"I have no idea."

"Have you listed any of his basketball team as failing?"

"No."

There was a knock on the door and Kyle Roberts, the social studies teacher, poked his head in. He said, "Sir, the boys in the gymnasium said Coach Jolly came in, paced around his office for a few minutes, then left. His car is not in the teacher's parking lot."

"Thank you, Mr. Roberts."

The principal waited for Kyle Roberts to shut the door before saying, "Mr. Stout, you're face is swelling, and by tomorrow morning that eye will be a deep purple. I think you should take the day off while I find out what's going on."

Heck lightly shook his jaw with thumb and forefinger, then probed over the puffy swelling under his right eye. It was a good thing he was an academic because he sure as hell was no fighter.

Heck's boss said, "Would you please write down a list of instructions for a substitute teacher? I'm sure Coach Jolly flew off the handle for some stupid reason. He'll apologize the next time he sees you. In the meantime, enjoy the day off, wear an ice-pack to keep the swelling down, and be back Thursday acting like nothing happened. That is, unless you want to press charges."

Heck said, "No. I'm not upset with Jolly. I don't think we've ever had a conversation. However, I would like to know his reason for embarrassing me in front of my future students."

"Thank you for not pursuing the matter. I'll make sure Jolly gives us a full accounting. Would you like for me to drive you home? I know you always walk to school."

"That would be great. If I walked home looking like this I'd get a hundred inquiries as to why I had just gone ten rounds with Max Schmelling."

CHAPTER 12—PAUL'S PAPER
Tuesday evening, October 19, 1943

For the past month and a half Paul had read everything he could find on philosophy. Mr. Stout opened a window for Paul and now things Paul had always taken for granted appeared in a new light. He craved intelligence and wisdom and he wondered if he had time to make up for all the years he had held those attributes in low esteem. He wanted to make an "A" in philosophy more than anything. He also wanted to impress Sarah with his ability to switch horses in mid-stride. No longer would he be a commodity like a paid mercenary or a gladiator. He wanted people to ask him to explain difficult concepts, to be an expert in something with an intellectual bent.

His paper was on Diogenes—the man in the pot. And while he had located some information in the library, he had not yet written anything down. Now Mr. Stout wanted an outline and a brief summary. He looked at the books he had gathered and stacked on the kitchen table. He thought he'd make a list of his sources first. From each book he wrote down the title, the author's name, the page numbers where he had gathered his information, and gave each listing an alphabetical designation.

On a second piece of paper Paul wrote the major categories of information he had accumulated. First was the general information of Diogenes' life prior to his arrival in Athens. Second, his training in Athens under Antisthenes. Third, a thorough analysis of his belief system. Fourth, how he lived his life according to what he believed. Fifth, how he influenced his fellow Athenian citizens. And sixth, what important aspects of philosophy, as it is practiced today, can be attributed to the legacy of Diogenes the Dog.

On an additional piece of paper he accumulated the various sayings attributed to Diogenes. Paul thought he would sprinkle these throughout his written text like gems waiting to be found by an adventurer.

Paul's mother peered over his shoulder. After reading his work and thumbing through some of the books she pulled out a chair and sat down. "What's she like?"

"Who, Mom?"

"The girl who's gotten a hold of my boy. The one who's made him abandon his adolescence. She must be something special."

"Her name is Sarah." Paul finished writing, added a period, and laid his pencil down. "But I'm doing this for me."

"You might think it's for you, but ultimately it's for Sarah. From all the romance novels I've read I have now become an expert on love. Just hear me out. You think your abilities at sports is a passing fancy and that she will only be impressed with something of more lasting worth. Money is not your problem because you and your dad make a fair amount of that and one day this ranch will be yours. You've decided that intelligence is her avenue of comparison and that's where you are most deficient. This philosophy is your way of saying, 'Hey, Sarah, look at me. Put me at the top of your list. I'm worthy of your attention.'"

"Mom, you might be right. But the learning of philosophy has opened my eyes to lots of things I was never aware of. I enjoy listening to Mr. Stout talk about what life is. How, over the centuries, smart people have tried to answer the important questions of what is real, how we can know it's real, and what we can do about it to live an authentic life. I'm learning that being ignorant is a choice, but it's not one you have to live with. I've changed that aspect of my life and I hope Sarah will realize there is more to me than being a stupid sports jock."

"Sounds good to me. When will we get to meet her?"

"Mom, right now she and I don't see eye to eye. It's going to take a while. Isn't it something how a life can change directions so fast? Two months ago I thought I knew everything. Now I'm aware that I know nothing."

"Son, you know your parents love you. And you know Sarah is a woman who stole your heart. I think those are two good things to start with."

CHAPTER 13—BRAD
Tuesday afternoon, October 19, 1943

Brad started looking through his papers. He didn't have many sources other than his textbook. The Epicureans had received liberal treatment and, unlike some of his fellow students who had had to dig for information, his was handed to him.

Brad thought he might like to lead a life like the one he was writing about. Do whatever makes you feel good and abstain from whatever does not. But making an outline of his paper and writing about the attributes of what distinguishes a follower of Epicurus was a daunting effort. He worried about maintaining his "D" average. He wasn't failing, but he wasn't far from failing. A bad grade on his paper might be the last nail in his coffin. He knew what he had to do.

"Hello, Mr. Rodriquez, may I speak with Inez." Brad realized that Inez was the only person he could count on to save his hide. Many times before he had come upon insurmountable requirements and, after an abysmal effort of his own, he habitually called Inez, who helped him make it to daylight.

"Hello, Brad. I'm so glad you finally called. The day is so late I had just about given up."

"Why would you have given up? It's still early. Mom said it'll be another hour before supper's ready."

"I know it's early this afternoon, but I was thinking in a bigger picture."

"I see. No, I don't see, but that doesn't matter. I thought you might come over and have supper with us tonight. Mom has fixed a pot roast and . . ."

"Brad, is there something you would like to ask me?"

"Yes. Yes, there is."

"Well, I know how shy you are and I'll be right up front with you. I'd be happy to."

"You would?"

"Sure."

"Well, come on over, Inez, and we'll talk about it."

Inez Garcia lived next door. She had been Brad's good buddy for several years. But while she felt inclined to have the relationship develop into something more like kissing on the front porch swing, Brad continued to think of her as a good friend, a confidant, someone ready to rescue him from the clutches of despair.

"You're going to ask me in front of your family?"

"No. You've already accepted, so we can dispense with the asking and get to the doing."

"I'll be right there."

Inez knocked on the Baker's front door before Brad had finished informing his mother that Inez would be coming for supper. Afterwards she would help him with his assignment in philosophy. Joyce, Brad's little sister, answered the door and walked into the kitchen with Inez. Joyce could smell the pot roast and wanted to swig a ladle of the stew juice.

"Hello, Inez. You look so pretty in yellow. I do believe yellow is your color."

"Thank you, Mrs. Baker. And thank you for inviting me for supper." Inez waited for Brad to say something.

"Inez, let's go onto the front porch. Dad is in the living room listening to the Cardinals playing baseball and he won't want us talking while Haray Caray calls the play-by-play."

"I have no problem with that."

On the way to the front porch Brad picked up his philosophy textbook and his clipboard with blank sheets of paper pressed under a strong spring. He followed a few steps behind. "So, do you know anything about hedonism?"

Inez stopped in her tracks. She turned to face Brad, who hadn't stopped and they clashed bodies. "Oh. I'm sorry, Inez. Here, let me get the door for you." Brad held the door for a suddenly depressed young lady.

They sat on the porch swing and started rocking back and forth. Inez pushed off with her feet. Brad thumbed through his book trying to locate the pages on hedonism and specifically how the followers of Epicurus had put it into practice.

"Okay, Brad, just exactly what do you want from me?"

"I thought you could help me get an outline for a paper I've been assigned to write and a brief summary of the full version we'll eventually write together. I'll treat you to a soda tomorrow afternoon at Eudy's."

"And . . ."

"And whatever else you think your efforts might call for."

"In that case, let's get started."

"Here, read these five pages and I'll get us glasses of lemonade."

"Brad, I've heard about this paper. You have to turn in a ten-page essay in a couple of weeks with the summary, outline, and sources due tomorrow."

"Yep."

"Brad, think about that. You're asking me to help you write ten pages based on five pages. Do you see anything wrong with that?"

"Nope. I have faith in you. You're the best."

"I am not the best, the most naive, maybe; the most gullible, definitely. But the best, probably not."

"Come on, Inez, we can do this. I'll make it worth your while."

"Yes, you'll do that. You will most certainly do that."

"Okay, read those five pages and I'll be right back."

When Brad went inside to get the beverages the telephone rang. He picked it up after one ring. "Baker's residence."

"Brad, this is Sarah. I've called to tell you that I'd be honored to accompany you to the homecoming dance."

"Gee, Sarah. That's swell. I'll get you a mum corsage from one of the pep club girls and pick you up at seven Friday evening. Dad said if I could get a date he'd let me drive the car."

"I gotta go, Brad."

"Okay, see you tomorrow."

Brad hummed a tune as he returned to the front porch carrying two glasses of a tart, freshly squeezed drink.

"Okay, let's break it down into two halves. The first half is the characteristics of Epicureanism. And the second half is how the followers implemented it in their daily lives. Then we'll break down each of those two halves into two more. The characteristics could be broken down first into how Epicureanism deviates from cynicism and the second into how it compares with stoicism. Now we can break down how the followers implemented it in their daily lives first for the individual, and second collectively for their society as a whole. For the summary you can write a short paragraph for each of the four topics"

"Inez, you are wonderful."

"That, I am. And capable of rude behavior, of crass vindictiveness, of deviant retaliation, and of outright retribution. Brad Baker, you don't want to take advantage of me. I can be your worst nightmare."

CHAPTER 14—HECK MAKES IT HOME
Tuesday night, October 19, 1943

When the principal dropped Heck at his doorstep, Heck looked around for evidence the kids were home. Through the kitchen window he saw them playing on the tire he had hung from a tree limb. May was swinging with Otis pushing her higher than Heck thought safe. He went to the back door and yelled at Otis to quit pushing May so high. At the refrigerator Heck scooped up a cup of ice cubes. What he needed now was something to hold the ice so he could strap it on the side of his face to stem the swelling. In a few minutes he had fallen asleep on the sofa with the ice sitting beside a lamp and melting in the cup.

At fifteen minutes after six Janice drove into the driveway. The Livery Feed and Seed was closer to their home than the school, but Heck insisted she take the car. He said he didn't mind walking. He usually had some potatoes peeled or a salad made when she arrived. Today it was almost dark, the kids were still playing in the backyard and no lights were on in the house. Janice walked in and dropped her purse before going around turning on lamps and closing window shades.

She saw her husband sacked out on the sofa. Thinking he must have had a hard day, she decided to let him sleep. She went into the kitchen and, through the back door, told the kids to come inside. Otis came holding a jar of dirt laced with night crawlers. "Mom, reach in and get one. I thought we'd fry him. You know, dip him in an egg batter, cake him down with crushed soda cracker, then stick him in the skillet. We could let Dad have the first bite."

"Otis, be quiet. Your dad's asleep."

"May, set the table. Tonight we're going to have leftovers."

Otis said, "Leftover from what? Now that you've started working we have leftovers five nights a week. I can't figure out where it comes from. The times we don't have leftovers we eat it all."

"Well, young man, aren't you the smart one."

"Yep. Get it from Dad. Don't you want to fix fried worms?"

"Do either of you have homework?"

"No," said Otis.

"Me, either. I never have homework."

"Then, May, that means you do all your assignments on the school's time."

"Mom, is that like the city's nickel?"

"I don't know. I guess it could be. Where have you heard that?"

"From Daddy. He goes out once a month with a big wrench and does something to the water meter. Then he comes back inside saying we're flushing on the city's nickel."

"Heck, Heck Stout, get yourself in here."

Heck heard his name and thought it was time for supper. He rose from a groggy stupor and walked a little crookedly into the kitchen. He sat down to an empty table. Janice and the children were wide-eyed at his appearance. With blood on his shirt, one side of his face swollen, and his eye painted in hues of purple and black, Heck looked ready for the trick-or-treaters.

Janice was instantly in front of her husband. "Honey, what happened to you?"

"Got pulverized by a barbarian in gym shorts."

"A student?"

"No, a teacher."

"You teaching teachers?"

"No. I don't know why he hit me. He called me a name and, wagging a finger in my face, said for me to leave his boys alone."

"And what are you doing to his boys?"

"Nothing. I don't even know who his boys are. Well, he teaches team sports so I guess he's the basketball coach and his boys probably play on the team. But I don't know what he's talking about. I'm not flunking anyone, and he's won both games played so far this year."

"Let me have a look at how much damage he did. Didn't you tell him you wore glasses and it's not polite to hit an overweight man wearing glasses?"

"No, honey, I didn't think to tell him that."

Janice retrieved a cube of ice from the refrigerator and told Heck to stick it in his jaw and hold it there with his tongue. She then took out a package of hamburger meat and started making patties for supper. One small dab she rolled into an egg-shaped ball and told Heck to close his eye. She told him to hold it against the eye and the cheek just below.

"What's this gonna do?"

"I don't know, but my cousins always did it after one of them got into a scrape. Tomorrow we'll add some makeup and you'll be as good as new."

"The principal told me to take tomorrow off. He said he was going to make the coach apologize and for me to enjoy the day, but to be back on Thursday."

The telephone rang. "Hello, Mrs. Burkett. Yes he did, but doesn't know why. No, I don't think that would be a good idea. He's asleep right now. Okay, thank you. Good-bye."

"That was our landlord. She's heard about the incident and wanted to come by with her husband to get your side of the story."

"This thing shows signs of escalating," said Heck.

The telephone rang again. Janice picked it up and said, "Hello." Her eyes grew wide. She put her hand over the mouthpiece and whispered, "It's Reverend Colfax." Into the phone she said, "No. Well that's news to me. He can't come to the telephone right now. I'll tell him you called. Thank you so much." Janice hung up the telephone and unplugged it from the wall.

"Another well-wisher?"

"No. Another upset neighbor. Did you say you were an atheist?"

"No, I did not. That's the name he called me: 'A frigging atheist.'"

"Well, Mr. Stout, you've dug yourself a nice hole. You'll have to hide in the woods tomorrow because when everyone finds out you're not at school they'll come here looking for you—and wanting you to deny his accusation. This could be embarrassing for all of us." Janice started to fix supper while Heck mulled over his situation. She thought seriously about frying up something special for her husband and looked around for Otis's jar.

CHAPTER 15—ANOTHER OFFER
Tuesday night, October 19, 1943

Let's see. Sarah told Brad she'd let him know tomorrow if she would go to the homecoming dance with him. It probably means she wanted to wait one more evening for someone she really wants to go to the dance with to call. Sarah's a pretty girl and popular, but most of the boys I know have regular girlfriends. Paul sat in his chair for a long time thinking, but couldn't think of another boy Sarah had shown an interest in. He was sure she was waiting on him to call.

The basketball team played better and better all the time. Friday night they would pummel the team from Skunk Hollow. After he had showered and put on a sports coat and slacks, he would meet her at a pre-arranged location. They would walk in arm in arm to a hero's welcome.

Paul waited for his parents to go onto the front porch and sit in their rocking chairs. He listened to the night sounds before he took a dining room chair to the telephone. He dialed her number. Sarah picked it up after only one ring. That was a good sign. It meant she was sitting there waiting for his call.

"Hello?"

"Hello, Sarah. You working on your paper for tomorrow?"

"No, that's already done. Hold on. I'll get Mother."

"No. Hello, Sarah . . . Sarah. Damn."

"Hello, Paul. This is Mrs. Bingham. Is there anything I can do for you?"

"No, ma'am. I called to talk with Sarah and she decided, on her own, that I probably wanted to talk with you. Will you put her back on the phone, please?"

"My pleasure." Paul heard, "Sarah, darling, he wants to speak with you."

"I'm sorry, Paul."

"That's all right. I just wanted to invite you to the homecoming dance after Friday night's game."

After a short pause Sarah said, "I'm sorry, Paul. I already have a date. Thank you for asking though."

"Think nothing of it. Goodnight, Sarah." Paul hung up the telephone. "It wasn't me—she was waiting on someone else and he called before I did. Damn. Damn. Damn."

Paul looked at his stack of papers. He thought, "I should have called her first, then done the homework." A melancholic fog of despair enveloped Paul.

On the front porch Paul's mother said, "Frank, have you heard Paul say anything about a girl named Sarah?"

"No. Not a word."

"If he had said a word, would you remember?"

"Probably."

"I understand the Livery Feed and Seed has received some new saddles with silver conchos from Fort Worth."

"They have?" Frank looked out into the night. All he could hear was the cicadas and his wife's chair rocking. Presently he said, "They have not. I was in there this afternoon."

"Exactly. You pick up on the things that interest you and don't even know when Paul or I have a birthday."

"You had a birthday?"

"No. But if I had, would you have remembered?'

"Did I remember your last one?"

"No."

"The one before that?"

"No."

"When is your birthday?" After a moment of silence he said, "Would you like a new saddle?"

"Frank Mitchell, I may have to whip you."

CHAPTER 16—SARAH RECONSIDERS
Tuesday night, October 19, 1943

Sarah went into her bedroom and lay down on the bed fully dressed. She had to think. Why did Paul wait so long before asking her to the dance? She had given him ample opportunity. There were the times she loitered around her desk after the bell, ran in the hallway so she could overtake him and step in front, and even cut in line. It's a wonder he hadn't knocked her down before he got his speed adjusted or yelled unfair when she slid in unexpectedly. And then tonight, just three days before the game and the dance. How long should a woman have to wait? When she thought she couldn't hold off any longer she'd called her ace in the hole. Brad was a nice guy, maybe a little boring, but he was someone who would do his best to make sure she enjoyed the evening.

"Paul, someone needs to give you a helping hand. Someone needs to tell you, 'Mr. Basketball Star, Mr. Class Celebrity, this is how you interest a woman. This is how you treat a woman. Mr. Good-Looking Guy this is how you grab the woman you love and show her what she's been missing.'"

Sarah thought of several scenarios that would culminate in her calling Paul to say there had been a new development and, indeed, she could now accompany him to the dance. Let's see. Brad could get sick, break a leg, have to make an emergency trip somewhere. He could call her and say "Sarah, I'm so sorry, but something has come up and, will you forgive me—I can't take you to the dance Friday night."

Sarah thought there might be something she could do to get out of her agreement. She could say, "Brad, Paul needs me. He doesn't think he'll be able to play basketball for worrying about me going to the dance with someone else. You need to give me up for the school."

Sarah thought she would call Inez and see if she could come up with a scenario that would work. "Hello, Inez. This is Sarah."

"Sarah, don't tell me you need help with your philosophy paper."

"No. I got that covered."

"Good, because I'm philosophized out. So what's going on?"

"I need some advice. There is this boy I wanted to ask me to the homecoming dance and he piddled around waiting to the very last minute before finally calling. In the meantime I accepted from someone else. Now I'd like to dump Someone Else and call back The Procrastinator and accept his invitation. Can you think of a way I could do that?"

"Sarah, do you think I can perform miracles?"

"Like no one else I know.."

"Okay, I'll accept that. Let's look at it from The Procrastinator's viewpoint. He waited until the last minute to ask the woman he really wanted to go with. Now, if he's going to the dance at all, he'll have to pick from the girls who have not been asked. There's not many of them." Inez knew of only one girl not yet asked. How would she handle being asked by someone she didn't know. Wait a minute, there wasn't anybody she didn't know

"Say, I've got it. Double date. Help him get a date with a friend of yours who has not been asked then both couples can share the same table. You can sit with Someone Else on one side and The Procrastinator on the other. Make polite conversation with both but be overly friendly with The Procrastinator. Smile, wink a few times, stare him down. Then, after a few dances with the boy who brought you, have your girlfriend ask Someone Else to dance. You can sit at the table with The Procrastinator and talk. Of course with the noise and the band playing, you'll have to have your face almost touching his so that he can hear what you're saying. Reach down and hold his hand. If he asks you to dance toy with the locks of his hair, pull on his earlobe, or run your hand under his jacket. Your girlfriend will be doing the same thing to Someone Else. Over the course of the evening, you and your friend could slowly trade partners without either of the two boys becoming aware of what's going on."

"Inez, you are incredible. How do you do it? You ought to head straight to Hollywood after graduation and write for the movies."

"Yes. That's exactly what I plan on doing. In the meantime I'm the girl who hasn't been asked who would love to take Someone Else off your hands."

"Okay, Inez. Tomorrow I'll talk to The Procrastinator and see if I can get things arranged."

CHAPTER 17—PICKETING
Wednesday morning, October 20, 1943

When Amos Considine, the Dancing Deer High School Principal, arrived at school for a routine day of principaling, three women held signs parading up and down the sidewalk in front of the school's administrative offices. He slowed his car enough to have time to read two of them. *No atheist teaches my child* on the first and *Cast out the demon* on the second.

"Man-oh-man, I got to do something. In a few minutes the newspaper will be here to take pictures. That damn Jolly." Amos parked his car in his reserved parking space and hurried to his office through the back door. On his way past his secretary Amos said, "Have the custodian deliver three of our most comfortable chairs out front and call the cafeteria. I want a plate of sweets and coffee delivered on a serving table to the women protestors pronto. Send someone into town if the cafeteria can't come up with the doughnuts. Pay for it from the petty cash box. Get Jolly in here right now."

In ten minutes the ladies out front sat in lawn chairs drinking coffee or tea. And Coach Jolly waited in the outer office for Amos to get off the telephone. "Yes, sir. I agree. I'm putting a lid on everything as we speak. No, sir. You won't have to come down here. I can handle it. Thank you, sir. Yes, I'll keep you informed. Yes, sir. Good bye, sir."

Amos pressed the button on his intercom and told his secretary to send in Coach Jolly. "Sit down, Jolly. Now, tell me what happened."

"We've got the homecoming game Friday night against Skunk Hollow and I've been working my boys till they can't stand up. Then Paul Mitchell leaves a note on my chair saying Stout gave him an assignment that takes precedence over basketball. He can't practice with the team. So I went looking for Stout. When I found him I punched his lights out and told him to leave my boys alone."

"Do you think that was the proper thing to do?"

"Amos, this is Stout's first year teaching. I've been here ten years. Don't you think I deserve a little respect? This will be our best year ever. We might even make it to the state championships. And you think I'm going to let a Mr. Nobody derail my efforts? There ain't no way. He deserved what he got and I ain't backing down."

"Mr. Jolly, you won't have to back down. But you will have to make a public apology and say you let your temper get the best of your judgment. You should not have stooped to being physical with a fellow teacher and you had no cause for name-calling."

"I ain't gonna do it."

"Mr. Jolly, you will do it or you will be in non-compliance with your contract."

"Amos, you can't do this to me. We're friends. We've been fishing together. Taken our wives on vacations together. Is this any way to treat your best friend?"

"I'm sorry, John, but I can't let you jeopardize my job like you're jeopardizing yours. I just got off the telephone with the school board superintendant. I promised him I would soon have everything under control. Now you either do what I say or clean out your locker and vacate the premises."

"You offering a severance package or anything?"

"I'll give you a month's pay. Now go think about it while I mollify these distraught mothers."

After Coach Jolly left, Amos walked to his window to see how the three ladies were behaving. "Whoa, where'd all the women come from?"

Amos stuck his head out his office door and said, "Where's those doughnuts?" At that moment the attendance clerk charged through the hallway door with sacks in both hands. "Here, give them to me", Amos said. "I'll deliver them myself. Have more chairs brought into my office along with two coffee pots and a dozen coffee cups with cream and sugar."

Amos Considine adjusted his pants, looked in the mirror to see if his hair was in place and walked out the front door bearing gifts for the Mongol Horde now holding his school siege. "Ladies, come into my office and let's discuss your terms. Here, have a doughnut. There's been a colossal misunderstanding. Would you like one with sprinkles or— here's one covered in chocolate. Yes, ma'am, I have more coffee inside.

Here's one with coconut. Ma'am, would you like a doughnut covered in coconut? I think there are éclairs in the bottom of the sack."

Inside his office, Amos asked his secretary to step inside to take notes. "Okay, ladies. I understand you're upset because one teacher called another teacher a name."

"It wasn't just a name. Coach John Jolly said that Mr. Stout was an atheist. Then he leveled the heathen."

"So, if Mr. Stout was a Jew it would have been all right?"

The spokeswoman looked around the room and seeing a few heads nod she said, "We are not discriminating against the Jewish faith. But that's not what he called him."

"Okay, what if he was an American Indian with a Ph. D. in Philosophy from the University of Utah. Would you let him lecture your children if he wore a headdress?"

"Don't be preposterous. We would not consider an Indian a threat to our children's well-being. I have Pawnee blood in my family line. That's fairly common in these parts. What's more, the Cherokee Indians traveling on the Trail of Tears wintered not far from here before continuing to Oklahoma."

"All right, say he was from Morocco and wore a fez. Do you think he might have something he could teach us?"

"Uh, I don't know."

"Okay, supposing he had written books on the subject he was teaching, had as much education as a person can get, and was loved by every single student in his class."

"Who are you talking about? Is this the same man?"

"Yes, ma'am. Heck Stout has written two books I'm aware of and has received his Doctorate in Philosophy from the University of Arkansas. We have no other teachers in any field of study who have the credentials Mr. Stout has."

"Well, we weren't aware of those facts."

"And you are telling me that, being Christian, you ladies can tolerate someone who believes in a competing deity to our God, the Father, but cannot tolerate someone who does not believe in any god at all?"

"That's exactly what we're saying."

A round of "Amen, Sister" and "You betcha" filled the room.

"How about if we get an apology from Coach Jolly? Here's more sweets. Does anyone need their coffee refilled? So Mr. Jolly says he flew off the handle and had no reason to call Mr. Stout an atheist."

"And Mr. Stout affirms he is not an atheist."

"Would you be satisfied then?"

"Yes, sir. We would."

"I would."

Several people said, "Me too." at the same time.

"All right, ladies, give me till ten o'clock Friday morning and I'll meet with you again in the gymnasium. Bring your friends. Maybe we can have some socializing afterwards."

The ladies left the principal's office feeling empowered by their collective effort.

CHAPTER 18—PLAYING HOOKY
Wednesday, October 20, 1943

Heck slept in on his day off. That is, he slept in until the telephone started ringing. The first call was from Mrs. Whipple. Heck didn't know who Mrs. Whipple was, but soon found out she knew who he was. He did a little stammering, a little clearing of his throat, and offered a few half-hearted interjections of "but", "no", "yes", "maybe", and "well." When she had finished her tirade the receiver went dead as she awaited his reply.

Heck said, "Yes, ma'am, Mr. Stout is not here at the moment. I'll be sure and give him your message. Goodbye, Mrs. Sniffle."

In less than five minutes the telephone rang again. Heck answered the phone in a falsetto voice saying he was the housekeeper. He said Mr. and Mrs. Stout were at their country estate for the rest of the week, but he was taking appointments for them. The following Monday was completely booked, but ten-thirty on Wednesday was free. When he finished nothing spewed from the receiver, so Heck asked the caller to call back if he decided to take the Wednesday appointment. Heck unplugged the telephone in time to hear someone pounding on his door.

From behind a bedroom curtain Heck peeked out to see a stout middle-aged woman whacking his door with an umbrella handle while a tall gaunt woman egged her on. He went into the kitchen and started a pot of coffee while listening to the women grow more and more agitated. Back at the window, Heck watched as they eventually grew weary of the ordeal and gave his door one last kick before throwing something into the bushes and marching in a heated storm to their car.

Heck noticed there was a lot more traffic going past his house than what he considered normal. He went into the kitchen, poured a cup of coffee, and wondered what the two women had thrown in the bushes. From the toaster he retrieved a pair of lightly toasted slices of bread and began spreading sweet butter topped with a generous helping of his wife's mayhaw jelly.

With one hand cradling two slices of toast and his other barely holding an extremely hot cup of coffee, Heck opened his front door and went to see what treasure he might find in the bushes.

It was his newspaper. They had thrown his delivered copy of the *Marsden County Meteor* among the rosebushes. Heck snaked a naked arm through a thorn encrusted entanglement, losing only one of the two pieces of toast before he hooked the paper with his smallest finger. With the newspaper, his one piece of toasted breakfast, and half a cup of coffee, Heck thought he might have a quieter morning hiding in the shed.

Heck opened a side door. He heard a low growl from Otis's spaniel before turning on a single bulb. Hell, even dogs hate atheists. Heck shared his toast with the mutt and opened a lawn chair. He might just take a nap. From a cardboard box stuffed at the back of a high shelf, he retrieved a mason jar of moonshine. He had found the cache of forbidden treasure when first moving in, but this was the first time he seriously thought of partaking. He didn't feel like answering questions posed by nosey neighbors. Maybe he would see if it was rotgut or something a little more palatable.

CHAPTER 19—SKUNK HOLLOW
Wednesday, October 20, 1943

Coach Jolly arrived at the Skunk Hollow high school. It was a beautiful day for treasonous activity. Sitting in his car he vacillated between setting things right while tucking his tail and sticking to his guns. If he did the former he would have to apologize to Amos, to Stout, to most of the mothers in Dancing Deer, and to his boys. Was he a man or a mole? Jolly grabbed a notebook, adjusted his tie, and trodded to the Philistine powerhouse.

"Have a seat, Mr. Jolly, and I'll go find our principal, Mr. Boynton. He left a few minutes ago saying he was headed to the gym. Are you and your boys ready for the big game? It's all anybody around here is talking about."

"Maybe I could mosey down to the gym. I'd like to see your facilities."

"Yeah, sure. Just follow the big hall to the left. It ends at the gym. If you go right, you end up at the cafeteria." Mr. Boynton's secretary pinned a visitor's pass on Coach Jolly's jacket and held the door to the hallway for him.

"Thank you, ma'am."

Coach Jolly had only made it as far as the library when classroom doors opened and students poured through. They all turned left and joined him on his walk to the gym. Some pushed and others shoved as lots of individual conversations and general rambunctiousness filled the hall.

At the end of the wide corridor both doors to the gymnasium were propped open to admit students four abreast. Jolly stepped to one side and let the throng pass. He peered into the confines of the gym to see banners hung on the walls. Skunk Hollow was in a fever. This was playing right into his hands.

Another teacher walked over to Coach Jolly and held out his hand.

"I'm looking for the principal. The woman in his office said he would be in the gym."

"Jim Blanchard." They shook hands. "The big guy's here all right. He and the coach will speak to the students in a minute. They're trying to stir up enthusiasm for the game, but I don't think it's necessary. The students are in a frenzy as it is. We got the biggest game of the year Friday night. And our boys are on a roll. They've won both of their games so far this season by lop-sided scores. If they can get a win against Dancing Deer nothing can hold them back from the state championships. Come on, let's go inside and see what they have to say. You can catch him after the pep assembly is over."

Jim Boynton led Coach Jolly to a cordoned area where the teachers congregated close to the door. Jolly took a seat and watched five young ladies yell, at the top of their voices, something incoherent and syncopated with the pumping of pom poms. Whistles, cheers, clapping, and pandemonium accompanied the five girls gyrating, bouncing up and down, and doing acrobatic routines for the pleasure of a gym full of people who hated Dancing Deer.

A man strode to a microphone standing as a lone sentinel in the middle of a hardwood floor. "Students, take your seats."

The audience clapped as the five young ladies finished their routine and hundreds of students scrambled to find chairs.

"We playing basketball this Friday night?"

The crowd roared, "Yes."

"Against anyone important?"

The crowd responded with a resounding, "No."

"Who's gonna win?"

"We are."

The cheerleaders started another routine, this time to a band accompaniment of Sweet Georgia Brown. One girl did a somersault and exhibited pink underwear for all to see.

"Let's have the basketball team come out."

The crowd clapped again as a dozen young men made it through the crowd to the microphone. One boy adjusted the microphone to his height. "I just want to say, me and the boys will be taking care of business Friday night." He had to wait for his jubilant classmates to calm down before continuing with, "and we want to publicly announce that we guarantee that when we leave the floor after the fourth period, we will have a victory in our back pockets."

He stepped back from the microphone. Coach Jolly spent the whole of the speech observing a shy young man even taller than Tall Paul. The young man shifted from one foot to the other obviously embarrassed about being put on display. Their coach stepped forward. He said, "After this game is over, Dancing Deer will be shaking their heads wondering what had just happened to their high and mighty basketball team. We plan on putting a damper to their homecoming festivities."

Students jumped from their seats and yelled at maximum volume. They threw pre-packaged confetti high into the air. The cheerleaders did another routine showing more pink underwear and the gymnasium started to look like a pre-war political rally in Berlin. When the Skunk Hollow principal made it to the microphone, the students calmed down. Each took a seat as he or she awaited some brilliant observation from the head cheese.

"I have no doubt that our boys will make good their guarantee. I want Skunk Hollow to prevail just as much as you do, but I also want to do it the right way. No underhanded tricks, no unsportsmanlike behavior, no retaliation for unintended offenses. Students, you represent the best of Skunk Hollow and I want everyone to understand how important it is to exhibit good conduct. If you lose, keep your head up and understand that it's not winning or losing, but how you play the game that matters. And if you win, don't gloat over your opponent's misfortune. Take everything in stride." Mr. Boynton had to wait for the applause to die down. His students were a bit unruly and susceptible to indecent behavior, but a word from him ought to change that.

"Now, with that said, I want to add that I have made a small side wager with the principal of Dancing Deer. So Monday morning if you see a man wearing a suit cleaning out trash cans, mopping floors, and serving food in the cafeteria, he will be my counterpart from our neighboring school. Don't taunt him. Treat him with all the respect he deserves. He has only placed his allegiance behind a losing force.

"Okay, it's time to head back to class. Remember, no running in the hallway. But first these lovely young ladies will entertain us once more with a special routine dedicated to the Skunk Hollow basketball team."

After the pep assembly dissipated and the students started heading for the exits, Coach Jolly lingered outside the double doors to keep an eye on the principal. After most of the students had left, Coach Jolly walked back inside and headed straight for the man he came to see.

He held out his hand. "Coach Jolly, from Dancing Deer."

The principal furrowed his eyebrows and turned his head sideways. "Pleased to meet you, Mr. Jolly. I'm Bob Boynton. What can I do for you?"

Coach Jolly squeezed the package tucked under his arm. "No, sir, it's what I can do for you."

CHAPTER 20—SUCCEEDING DANCES
Wednesday, October 20, 1943

"Sarah, have you spoken to The Procrastinator?" asked Inez as she shifted books from one arm to the other.

"Relax, Inez, he's in my first class. The day has just started, why are you in such a hurry?"

"Because I haven't been asked, I have never been asked, and I'm afraid I'll never be asked. That's why."

"Inez, you are a paradox. The smartest girl I know and very pretty in a cute sort of way. You should have received several invitations."

"That's true. You'd think I was invisible or something. Do you have any ideas?"

"Well, I don't want to hurt your feelings. Have you talked it over with your mom? My mom and I have talks like that all the time. Other than you she's my best friend."

"Sarah, I have five brothers. My mom doesn't have time for me. It takes everything she can do to wash the clothes, cook the meals, and clean the house."

"Does she not mow the yard as well?"

"No. I have five brothers to do that—but come to think of it, Joey is the only one who mows the yard. Joey's the youngest. Most of the time his older brothers are tearing an engine apart to see how it works. Collectively they've taken six engines apart and can't get any one of them back together. I thought about telling them how to place the pieces on their worktable leading out from the block. Then when they'd cleaned each part or repaired or replaced it they'd have to put it back in the exact same spot. When it was time to reassemble, they'd start with the furtherest part and work back to the block from there."

"But you didn't?"

"Naw. Let them waller in their own mud. But if you have any ideas on why I never get asked out I promise not to take offense. I really do need some help. I'm past being picky. Its gotten so bad I thought about taking out an advertisement in the *Marsden County Meteor.*"

"That's a little drastic, don't you think?"

"Just the musings of a near hysterical high school girl who's never been kissed."

"Inez, let's talk about it in our gym class. Here's my first-period room." Sarah opened the door to Mr. Stout's classroom and sat in her seat before noticing the substitute teacher. She looked around to see if Paul was there yet.

Paul took long strides down the hall trying to make it to class on time. He had an armload of books and a sheaf of papers to turn in. Still quite a ways from his class door a girl who had been waiting on him stepped from a dark doorway directly in his path.

Sliding to a halt prior to running into the out-of-place female Paul said, "Whoa. Sorry, Laney. Can't talk right now; I'll be late to class. Laney, what's with the tears?"

"Paul, will you take me to the homecoming dance?"

"Have you and Andrew had an argument? Is that what the tears are for?"

"No, Paul. Andrew isn't talking to me, but we haven't had an argument."

"Then why is he not talking to you?"

"Paul, it's a long, sad story. Will you listen to me tell you about it at lunch? It's warm enough we could meet outside. Paul, I'm desperate."

"Sure. Okay. How about we get something portable from the cafeteria? We can meet by the path to the band room. If one of us gets there early enough, a bench will probably be available."

"I'll see you there. Paul, you're the best."

When Paul entered his Mr. Stout's classroom, people were already seated and in the process of sending yesterday's assignment to the front. A new teacher had taken Mr. Stout's place and collected the proffered papers.

"Class, according to Mr. Stout's notes I'm supposed to lecture on the death of Antony and Cleopatra and the burning of the great library at Alexandria. I don't think Mr. Stout is aware that substitute teachers usually babysit while the students do something to prepare for the regular teacher's return. However, I do know a little about Greek tragedy and can provide a lecture of sorts in that arena. Have any of you heard the story of Oedipus Rex?" The substitute teacher looked about the room but no hands showed.

"Okay, Oedipus Rex is a Greek play about a man who was destined to fulfill a prophesy. He was to kill his father, marry his mother, and sire four children."

There were gasps, a few groans, and Brad Baker put his head in his hands. Between classes, Paul learned of the altercation between Coach Jolly and Mr. Stout. He heard that Coach Jolly had cleaned out his office and no one had seen him since he stormed out thirty minutes after knocking Mr. Stout to the ground.

Paul leaned against someone's locker as students whizzed past on their way to second period. Like Brad, Sarah, and several others, Paul had his first two classes in the same room. He looked at his watch and realized he still had three minutes before the bell sounded saying, "You should be arriving at your classroom." He gazed down the hall and wondered what had caused the ruckus everyone was talking about. How was this going to affect the basketball game and the homecoming festivities? Why had life become so difficult?

"Paul, I'm sorry I wasn't able to accept your invitation. If you haven't asked anyone else I have a friend who needs a date and the four of us could sit together."

"What? Oh, I'm sorry, Sarah, what did you say? I was deep in thought."

"I asked if you had a date for the homecoming dance."

"Not yet. The girl I really wanted to ask had other plans. But there's still two days. That gives me one day to ponder the problem and one day to be serious about it. Then there's always the two hours before the game and the hour between the game and the dance. I'm not worried yet."

"Paul Mitchell, a girl can't wait forever."

"You are so right. And some boys don't take rejection well. They have to be absolutely certain before they'll risk being turned down by a spoiled girl who's upset for having to wait."

"*Touché.*"

"So, do you know anything about this fight between Mr. Stout and Coach Jolly?"

"Not a thing. But let's go back to our talk about the dance. I have a friend who needs a date and then you and my friend could share a table with me and my date. Sort of like double-dating."

"No, I won't agree to that. I'll get my own date, thank you. I've been thinking about going to Skunk Hollow to bring back one of the girls from The Gilded Lily."

"That is so juvenile. Mr. Mitchell, we are through talking."

"Oh now, Sarah, I wasn't being serious."

"Paul, I'm having trouble figuring you out. I don't know when you're playing with my emotions or being deadpan earnest. I may have to take you under advisement and do a case study."

"I'll try not to disappoint. Will you save a dance for me?"

"Only under one condition. That I get to pick the song, the time, and the place for any succeeding dance."

"That doesn't sound all that bad unless—unless you don't like the way I do it and I spend the rest of my life waiting for a second chance."

"Then you better make that first one a crackerjack."

The bell rang and the students loitering in the hall poured into the classrooms. Once more seated, Sarah wondered just how deep Paul Mitchell was. She'd noticed lately his vocabulary had changed. He came up with new and intriguing questions for Mr. Stout. Was Paul Mitchell the man for her? He was sure a handsome guy. Her heart speeded up whenever he was around and she wasn't able to stop staring when he was in her field of vision.

Sarah and Inez had gym class for third period. In the girls locker room Sarah changed into a pair of disgustingly out-of-style, loose-fitting gym shorts with each leg billowing out before abruptly ending in thigh-hugging elasticity. The two girls wandered onto the shiny hardwood gym floor hoping no one of the male gender was in attendance. Sarah said, "The Procrastinator told me he could get his own date, thank you very much. So I guess our plans have been foiled."

"Sarah, that is not good news. But I have one last card I've been holding back. I think it's probably time I trump the pile."

At lunch Paul bit into an apple while Laney told him about her problem. "Paul, I'm pregnant."

"Really?"

"Yes. It's pretty well confirmed and Andrew is not the father. We've only been dating for this last month. It has to be someone else."

"And you don't know who?"

"Right. I've not been very picky. I told Andrew it wasn't his. Now he won't have anything to do with me."

"Laney, you would not be the best date for a man wanting to keep a pristine reputation intact."

"Paul, I'm the homecoming queen. I have to have an escort."

"I know, Laney, but what about your other boyfriends? Couldn't you ask one of them?"

"No. I only dated most boys once or twice and then I broke up. It was always so messy. For other girls, it's the boys who don't want a steady relationship. They flit from one girl to the next, but for me I always found the boys lacking. After two dates, I was usually bored."

"I see."

"It wouldn't be like you'd have to dance every song with me. Once I get seated I can take care of myself. You get a beverage, dance every so often with me, and take me home. In between times, I wouldn't mind if you went around the room and danced with other girls."

"All right, Laney. But after the dance we're going straight home. I'll be dead tired after the game and I have to get up early Saturday morning for chores."

"It's a deal. I'll even get my own mum."

"And you'll have to get a ride there. I have to be in the gym two hours before the game starts."

"No problem."

CHAPTER 21—COMPOUNDING PROBLEMS
Wednesday, October 21, 1943

When lunchtime rolled around Inez located Brad and got into the serving line at his side. When it was her turn she picked up a tray and set it on the shelf in front of a glass partition. Just like Inez's mannerisms were obstacles separating her, the glass partition separated the food from sniffling, coughing, or spitting students who might intentionally or accidentally adulterate it. Adding a napkin and flatware she pushed her tray forward. "Brad, I want you to take me to the homecoming dance."

"Inez, I've already got a date."

"You do?"

"Yep. And I've already turned in my paper so you can't snatch it back."

"You owe me, Brad. Tell your date a catastrophe has come up and you can't take her to the dance. If you do your family will be sold into slavery and seven plagues will be unleashed on mankind."

"That's funny, Inez. You've always been funny but not very practical. I can't do that. Sarah's your best friend—other than me."

"You're Someone Else?"

"Someone Else? Inez, I don't understand."

"You don't have to. I now have a plan. Hang in there, Brad, you'll soon learn what you have to do. It might not be pretty. You might not like it. But then again, no one cares what you think."

"Inez, why do you talk to me as if I'm a simpleton? I have feelings and you constantly trample on them. I'm taking Sarah to the homecoming dance, and that's that."

"Brad, you're such a dear. I sometimes get carried away with my own sense of self-worth. I don't mean to talk down to you. I guess I thrive on getting myself into the worst possible predicament just to see if I can figure a way out."

Inez picked up a glass of iced tea at the end of the serving line and headed to a table. Brad had opted for milk. The cafeteria was full of noisy students separated into groups. Things like common interests, class standing, and popularity grouped them—however, it was mostly popularity. Inez and Brad looked for Sarah. Everyone knew Sarah was the prettiest girl in school and Inez was the smartest. Brad was thankful that he was sometimes allowed to sit with them.

"Inez, why don't you have a date?"

"I don't know. Why didn't you ask me?"

"I was afraid of your commentary on me overreaching my station. You spend a lot of time telling me where you are and where I should be."

"I see. Well, Brad, all that's gonna change. From now on you're gonna see a new Inez. A more lovable, a more interesting, a more companionable Inez." With that said, Inez rose from her seat, walked around the table, and kissed Brad on the mouth. She kissed him right there in front of the entire class. The room was full of activity and petty conversations so few people noticed.

Brad was speechless. He watched with keen interest as Inez walked around the table back to her seat. With a hand on her chair back Inez turned and said, "I'll be right back." She walked toward the end of the serving line where Sarah was picking up her food.

When Inez approached she said, "Sarah, I've just talked to Someone Else and if you'd like to tell The Procrastinator that you're free to go to the dance with him I think I can make Brad agree."

"That's great, Inez. I talked to him after first period and he didn't have a date so I have to find him before he lets it be known that he's looking. If that happens, I'll have to apply for an interview. Where are you sitting?"

"With Brad. I just kissed him."

"You did? In the cafeteria?"

"Yep. Sarah, you're looking at the new and improved Inez."

Together the two girls walked back to where Brad clutched his fork. He had already realized he was no longer in control. Other powers had usurped his position and he sat waiting to be told his destiny.

"Hello, Brad. You got any news about Mr. Stout or Coach Jolly?" Sarah set her tray down, then plopped herself down directly across from Brad and beside Inez.

"Only that no one has seen either one and Coach Jolly's office and desk have been cleaned out. The boys on the basketball team don't know who'll be coaching them. Some think the game will have to be canceled."

Inez put a napkin in her lap. "Has anyone tried to call Mr. Stout or Coach Jolly?"

"I haven't heard," said Brad.

Sarah said, "Someone will coach. Replacing a coach should be easier than replacing a star player, don't you think?"

"Sure, but I'd still like to know what each one has to say. Sarah, Brad tells me you and he are going to the dance together."

Sarah decided not to answer and took a bite of food.

Inez turned to Brad and said, "Sarah has a problem. She would rather go with another boy but accepted your invitation when he dallied about asking her. How about you and I going to the dance and letting Sarah go with the other boy?"

"Is that right, Sarah?"

Sarah had a mouth full of food and choked. Something went down the wrong channel and she couldn't get any air. Her face started to change colors, she tried to cough and held both hands now shaking out over her plate.

Brad continued to look at Sarah waiting for her to reply. Inez jumped up and, from behind Sarah, Inez thumped her back with both palms. Sarah coughed, dislodged a particle of food, coughed some more, and dabbed at her eyes with a napkin.

"Inez, you haven't changed at all." Brad stood up and grabbed his tray. "Sarah, you can go to the dance with whomever you wish." Brad walked away.

In a moment Sarah felt better. She said, "Inez, that could have gone better."

"I know. I'm finding bad habits are hard to break. I don't know why I said what I did. I didn't want to hurt Brad's ego. Now I've got to figure out some way to minimize the collateral damage."

"Inez, your main problem is your compulsion to solve everyone's problems, whether they want your interference or not."

"So you would rather have choked to death?"

"No. In that single instance your interference was much appreciated."

CHAPTER 22—A NEW COACH
Wednesday, October 20, 1943

Amos Considine walked to the gym for the final period of the day. This was the period saved for team sports and would continue later into the evening after everyone else had gone home. When he walked onto the gym floor he noticed that none of the boys had changed into their gym shorts and t-shirts. They stood in three small groups talking in hushed tones.

"Gentlemen, let's have a meeting. Unstack some of those fold-down chairs and we'll discuss our options."

Soon, with everyone sitting but the principal, Amos said, "Coach Jolly is gone. He will no longer be coaching here. We have sent out notices for applicants to fill his position but it will be several days before any replies are received. Until we hire a replacement, I will fill in. I don't know much about basketball other than as a spectator so I want you gentlemen to more-or-less manage yourselves. We'll use the starting line-up from the previous game and hope your superior abilities without a proper coach can beat a less talented team with proper coaching. Does anyone have anything to add?"

A boy named Mark raised his hand. "Naw. We can beat Skunk Hollow without Jolly. He was more in the way than anything else."

"Okay, change clothes and let's practice. Is there any one who hasn't played yet?"

"I haven't." A rather short and scrawny kid held his hand in the air.

"Then you are now my assistant. Stay at my side and tell me everything that's going on and what I should do."

The Dancing Deer student body referred to the starters on the basketball team as the Five Apostles because they were Steve and James at guard, Andrew and John at forward, and Paul at center.

When the players reappeared on the floor, they were ready for practice. Amos looked down to his assistant, who said, "They should shoot baskets from varying distances for about ten minutes to warm up."

Ten minutes later Hayden, Amos' assistant, said Amos should stand beside the basket and, with each player running in from a line, he should toss the ball to the charging player. After making an easy layup each player should get back in line for another try. A few minutes later Hayden repositioned Amos to the other side of the basket and had him deliver the ball to a player circling around another player acting as an adversary. Next Amos bounced the ball behind the legs of the man guarding him to the Dancing Deer player advancing toward the backboard. After they did this for a while, the five starters took positions around the court and coordinated passing the ball while the remaining players tried to steal it. They ended the practice with a game of making shots from the free throw line. Ten shots in a row let a player head to the showers if all were made. Amos was there till almost dark before the last player, Tall Paul, made his ten straight baskets.

"Mr. Mitchell, I was told you are our best player."

"Sir, I can do everything except make free-throws."

That night Amos asked his wife if she knew anything about basketball. She answered, "No, dear. I go with you, but I spend my time seeing what the other women are wearing. And I wait until the finish of the second period so I can socialize."

The next day, Thursday, Amos started his day in the library to see if there was something on basketball for him to read.

CHAPTER 23—A NEW APPROACH
Wednesday night, October 20, 1943

After the evening meal, Betty Baker and her daughter, Joyce, cleaned up the kitchen while her husband, Johnston, turned on the radio and opened his paper. Brad retired to his bedroom to read about the sleuthing of Sherlock Holmes.

In a minute Joyce knocked on his bedroom door. "Is there a Don Juan here?"

"Don Juan? What are you talking about?"

"Inez and some other girl are at the front door asking if they can speak with the resident Don Juan. That can't be Dad."

"Tell them to have a seat on the porch swing. I'll be right out." Brad found his shoes and combed his hair. Maybe, he thought, he should put on a clean shirt. In a mirror he looked to see if he'd dribbled food down the front of the one he was wearing. Soon he was out of his room, looking as best he could, and headed to see what this Don Juan business was all about.

"Hello. Do I need to bring my mother out to even up the odds?"

Inez said, "She'd be on our side and you'd be even more outnumbered. Here, have a seat." Inez scooted to one side of the swing and Sarah scooted to the other, leaving the middle open for Brad.

"I think I should go inside for another chair. You know—give me an escape route."

"Brad, you don't need to escape from us."

"Do I need fighting room?"

"No, we don't want to fight either. We want to make a deal. You could come out of this the envy of all the other boys in school."

Brad sat down between the two girls. However, he remained on his guard, expecting something unpleasant to develop. "I don't know. This has the makings of some dreadful karma."

Sarah put her chin on Brad's left shoulder and her arm on his right while Inez held his hand. Inez said, "Brad, I want to apologize for being so rude to you at school. Sarah and I have been talking and she told me some things I do that upset other people. I'm going to try my very best not to be like that anymore." Sarah put her hand on the back of Brad's head. With her elbow resting on his left shoulder she began twirling his hair around a finger. Brad turned to see what Sarah was up to, then back as Inez continued. "Brad, we want you to take both of us to the homecoming dance." Sarah leaned forward. She placed her chin on Brad's left shoulder a second time.

Brad squirmed in his seat. "Both?"

"Yep. Sarah will ride in the middle on the way to the dance and I'll ride in the middle on the way back. You have to dance with both of us. You know—take turns."

"I don't know if I've got enough money for two girls. There's the tickets for the basketball game, tickets for the dance, mums for each girl, refreshments, and pictures by the photographer."

Sarah said, "Brad, Inez and I can help you with the finances. We want you to have as good a time as we will be having."

At that moment the screen door opened a few inches, a hand placed a wad of money on a piece of cardboard, and shoved it toward the swing with a broom handle. Brad looked at the money and asked, "Is this a conspiracy? Is everyone here in cahoots?"

Sarah took her finger out of Brad's ear. Inez let go of Brad's hand and placed both hands in her lap. Sarah said, "Brad, we feel so bad about the way we talked to you at lunch we thought we might make it up to you in some way. You know, you might be the only boy there with a girl on each arm. And two girls not arguing about which one was preferred. Brad, after Friday night you might have the entire school thinking you are Don Juan reincarnated."

"Or ask me to foretell their future, thinking I'm Rasputin reincarnated."

"Brad Baker, you are just too funny. I think we'll all have a wonderful time. What do you say? You haven't got much to lose and so much to gain. But you will have to come up with a plausible reason for taking two girls instead of the customary one girl to the dance."

"You mean other than I was coerced by two attractive girls while I had my guard down?"

Later, when Sarah and Inez walked back to Inez's house, Inez asked, "Why do you think Paul asked Laney to the dance? I thought she was dating Andrew."

"I don't know. Maybe he tried to make a statement. Laney is awfully pretty and she is the homecoming queen."

"Yeah, I know. Do you have any idea how she wrangled that? No one I know voted for her. Most people say they voted for you."

"Well, I didn't get enough votes to even be one of her attendants."

"Yeah, both attendants were her best buds. I think there was some hanky-panky going on." After entering Inez's house Sarah called her mother to come and pick her up.

"Sarah, we ought to find out how Laney pulled it off. Whoa—let me think—she takes away the homecoming queenship from you and now steals away Paul. I think we got foul play here. What do you think?"

"Inez, you need to concentrate on the good in other people and let the nasty remarks wither on the vine. You remember what we talked about earlier. You know—the new Inez."

"I can't just let it go if I think a friend has been wronged."

"Yes, you can. Focus on the good things and be a gentle soul. Not a vindictive, manipulating, judgmental, conniving witch."

"I used to be like that?"

"Inez, you are my best friend. But sometimes you try my patience."

CHAPTER 24—THE INQUISITION
Thursday morning, October 21, 1943

Amos Considine came out of his office with his hand extended. "Heck, that eye looks good. Did it not swell or turn colors?"

"My wife showed me how to use her makeup for camouflage."

"Good. Your wife must be an expert. Come into my office. We've been waiting for you."

Heck entered the school's main administrative office and stood beside the only vacant chair. Besides the principal, his assistant and Everett Irving, the Marsden County District Attorney, were present.

"Mr. Considine, is this an inquisition? Am I being charged with something? Do I need a lawyer?"

"Certainly not. My assistant is here to write down the particulars so I can report back to the school board superintendent what we discussed. Emmett is here to answer any legal questions raised."

"What kind of legal questions?"

"In case you want to press charges against Coach Jolly or sue the school for being hurt on the job."

"Okay." Heck sat down and crossed his leg. "Did you get an explanation from Jolly?"

"Sort of. He was upset with you because one of his players thought it was more important to complete an assignment you had given than to practice with the team. He went looking for you and got madder with each step he took. He's no longer employed by the school."

"Who's going to coach the basketball team?"

"I've sent out some notices and expect to receive replies from neighboring high school assistant coaches within the next few weeks. Until then I'll fill in. That is, unless you know anything about basketball."

"No. Never played hoops."

"All right. Back to the main reason for the meeting. We held off making a statement to the paper. All we need is for you to sign this document. I'll get the paper and a few irate mothers up to speed and things will be almost back to normal."

"Let me see the paper."

Emmett took out a sheet of paper from his valise and handed it to Heck. As Heck looked over the paper one of Heck's eyes closed, the other squinted, and his lips pressed together showing a flat frown across his face. "I'm not signing this. My spiritual beliefs do not impugn my ability to teach and should not be a criteria on which my performance is judged."

"I can assure you neither I nor the school board nor the state care one iota what your religious persuasion is. We just want to mollify a few belligerent mothers."

"The city authorities of Athens told Socrates that if he did not apologize and say he would cease teaching in his accustomed manner he would be executed. The Universal Church told Galileo Galilei he had to tell the world he was wrong and, indeed, the sun rotated around the earth and not vice versa or he would be excommunicated and possibly burned at the stake. When he was not forthcoming with a positive reply they led him into the torture room. There were blood stains on the church's implements. He agreed to lie. So now, in a like manner, you want me to lie to the parents of my students or I will be relieved as their teacher."

"It's not the same thing."

"It is and I won't do it."

"Mr. Stout, we don't want to lose you. In my personal opinion you are the best teacher we have. But if we lose the confidence of the parents who send us their children, how do you think we can remain an instructive cog on the educational wheel?"

"I think that is something you'll have to figure out, Mr. Considine."

"Mr. Irving?"

"See here, Stout. We don't want no Scope's Monkey Trial in Dancing Deer. Sign the damn agreement and get back to doing what you do best."

"What I do best, Mr. Irving, is show my students how to live their lives in accordance with a high set of ethical standards. Setting those standards is one of the primary components of philosophy. If I were to sign your agreement I would be admitting I could be pressured into reneging on my personal ethics and what I hold most dear is really not all that important. It would undermine my ability to teach. No, sir, lets take this to a court of law and let my peers decide if I should be fired or not."

"That's exactly what we don't want to happen. The peers you suggest are the same ones who picketed the school yesterday morning. The ones who held up banners saying they didn't want an atheist teaching their children will be the same ones deciding your fate. Do you really want that? Can we not reach a compromise—something we both can live with?"

"What can you offer me?"

"I can give you three months salary and a letter of recommendation. You can take that letter and teach in any other public school—just not one in Dancing Deer."

"A year's salary and no interview with the paper."

"Heck, the paper is going to write something. How about you give them whatever information you want to supply and keep the school out of it. If you do that I'll see that you get a full year's salary and the letter."

"I'll think about it."

"The irate mothers are coming to the school in the morning at ten. I'm supposed to show them this letter or tell them the school's position. You can take until thirty minutes before the meeting."

CHAPTER 25—THE STATEMENT
Thursday Afternoon, October 21, 1943

Heck decided to take matters into his own hands and, in an aggressive mood, he opened the front door to the *Marsden County Meteor*. Heck told the receptionist he wanted to talk with Jesse Bell, the owner and editor of the paper.

In a few minutes he was ushered into Jesse's office and offered a comfortable chair. "Ah, Mr. Stout. This is a pleasant surprise."

"Hello, Mr. Bell. I am being terminated from my teaching position because I won't compromise my personal spiritual beliefs. The principal and Emmett Irving, representing the Board of Education, offered me a fair settlement if I would not press the issue and would clear the air by making a public statement with your paper."

"Mr. Stout, that is not good news. Everything I've heard about you is positive. Your students love you. You've made a difference in several lives and will leave a definite void should you persist in leaving. Would you reconsider if I spoke up on your behalf?"

"Thank you, Jesse, but I can't water down my standard of ethics. Amos Considine is positive that the mothers will not tolerate their children being taught by someone with a different set of beliefs."

"Just exactly how does your set of beliefs differ from the norm?"

"That's not the proper question. You should ask why should it matter."

"Okay, why should it matter?"

"It shouldn't. I don't teach my personal beliefs to the class. I teach world history exactly as it happened. Part of the curriculum involves Judaism, Christianity, Islam, Buddhism, and all the other religions. It overlaps into my second course, which is philosophy. And I teach philosophy exactly as it developed from its Greek beginnings to the present day. I do not color my lectures with my opinion nor do I have a personal agenda"

"I applaud your tenacious spirit, but you have to realize where you are and what you're up against. You're teaching in the middle of the Bible Belt with the people in our area predominately Christian. No, more than predominately, they are just about exclusively Christian. Until that changes, and I hope it never does, you will have to take their set of values into consideration and teach accordingly. No one should care what your belief system is as long as it remains with you and is not a focus in your classroom. But, now that the issue has been raised, how can we word it so no one takes offense and things get back to normal?"

"Exactly. How can we do that?"

Jesse bounced his pencil against a leather insert in his desk while he thought. Presently he said, "Heck, what will you do if you quit teaching for awhile?"

"I don't know. I wrote an introductory book on philosophy during my college days and almost finished a second. In France the new rage is Existentialism. I've thought about incorporating my ideas on that as the last few chapters of the second book."

"I heard you were called an atheist."

"Yes, I was. That was the basis for Mr. Considine's letter. They want me to deny the accusation and to affirm my belief in God the Father and Jesus Christ as our Savior in writing."

"Are you an atheist?"

"No. I'm more like an agnostic. I would believe if I could use my reasoning ability to prove it or if there were some basis for belief other than taking someone else's word for it."

"So the church saying so is not good enough and the Bible is just a book."

"Yes. I need evidence or some logical reasoning good enough to sway my opinion. But none of this has ever been brought up in class or in church—which I attend on occasion."

"You know, Mr. Stout, I think the best avenue for you is to let sleeping dogs lay. Let's not address the issue of your belief, or non-belief, in the Deity but instead say that you need to finish your book. You have decided that, to you, the book is more important than teaching. You are sorry for any inconvenience this may cause your students and you hope they will continue to study in the direction you had been leading."

"That sounds good to me. Thank you for your help, Jesse."

CHAPTER 26—LAST MINUTE PREPARATION
Friday, October 23,1943

Amos Considine walked through the gymnasium toward the boys' locker room. He thought this was going to be a wonderful plus for his resume. Not only had he successfully defused a major rift that threatened to alienate the Dancing Deer citizenry, but he was going to coach his boys to a homecoming victory against their arch rivals. His boys had easily defeated Pottsville and Scranton and now they would solidify their pre-eminence by trouncing Skunk Hollow. Amos didn't want to ever leave Dancing Deer. Still, he would certainly appreciate letters from larger cities wanting to lure him to a higher-paying district. He noticed that, with the game to start in an hour and a half, people were already getting seated. This would be a sell-out.

In the locker room his boys were getting dressed. Nice clothes they had brought to change into for the dance dangled on hangers; polished shoes sat in the bottoms of lockers; and billfolds, watches, and class rings huddled together on top shelves of each player's lockable compartment.

Andrew walked to the bench where Paul sat. "I need to talk to you about Laney."

"Andrew, you and I are friends. I'm only taking Laney to the dance because she said she didn't have a date. She's not my girlfriend, I'm just giving her an arm to enter on. Since I won't be there much you should sit at her table. She told me I could go around the room and dance with other girls."

"Yes. I figured as much. Did she tell you she was pregnant?"

"Yeah."

"Well, that's baloney. Laney makes up stories to get what she wants. The reason she's had so many boyfriends is that she treats the men in her life like we're inferior in some way. And she won homecoming queen because she told Howard he could take her to the dance if she did."

Paul thought for a moment and said, "And Howard, being the chairman of the homecoming committee, rigged the election?"

"Precisely. And arranged for her two compadres to be her homecoming attendants."

"Then why ask me? You still would have taken her, wouldn't you?"

"Sure. But she wanted to trade up and you are so single-minded about basketball you weren't aware of her reputation."

"I thought her reputation was of a tarnished woman easily led astray."

"No, that's not true. That's just a veneer to cover her deep-seated insecurity."

"Does anyone else know the part Howard's playing?"

"Just you and I. Howard is really a nice guy, but he has problems of his own. No one much cares for his company because he makes excuses. And he's more friendly than the situation calls for. He comes across as insincere with a bland personality. Still, he and Laney might make a fine couple."

"I'm glad you told me, Andrew."

"Think nothing of it. If we win this game it'll be because of you and I wanted you to know I've got your back."

Amos shouted in a loud voice. "When everyone gets dressed let's discuss the strategy we'll use to mop up the floor with these upstarts from down the road."

CHAPTER 27—WARMING UP
Friday, October 23, 1943

The center of the center section of bleachers was roped off so the queen and her court could sit in a place of prominence. The girls in the pep club sat in the left bleacher section with the seats left and right of the queen's area reserved for singles, couples, parents, teachers, and anyone else wanting to root for the boys from Dancing Deer. Directly in front were five young ladies grappling with pom poms bouncing up and down in rhythm with the music. Occasionally, when time to coax the fans into a screaming frenzy, they replaced the pom poms with large hollow cones they used as megaphones.

Across the floor, another complete set of bleachers caged the Skunk Hollow fans. Sometimes a late-arriving Dancing Deer fan would not be able to find a seat on the home side but could across the floor. He had to be careful what he said to the invaders he sat with and also to not let his team and friends know he was among the enemy.

"Sarah, this is exciting. Do you know anything about basketball?"

"Very little. Mostly I watch them run up and down the floor while waiting for intermission."

"We need to know more than that. I think we could enjoy the game if we knew some of the rules. Did you buy a program?"

"No. I already know their names."

From the boys' locker rooms two groups of gladiators emerged. Dancing Deer took the right half-court under the scoreboard and Skunk Hollow took the left half-court in front of the Dancing Deer pep club. Each group of boys tossed their warm-up jackets aside before running onto the hardwood floor. They used ten or so balls to begin warming up by shooting baskets from varying distances and angles.

Inez said, "Sarah, do you notice anything different between our boys and theirs?"

"No."

"Well, they have more of them. And that one guy is taller than Tall Paul. Several are smaller than anyone on our squad. Why do you think there would be a need for having someone so short? After all, this is a tall man's game."

"I don't know, Inez. You're the analytical one. When you figure it out let me know."

"Also, the little guys aren't shooting baskets. They're playing keep-away. Now, some of them are running to the basket and tossing the ball up at the last minute with it bouncing off that board thing into the circular thingamajig."

"You know, Inez, I think you should get a job working for a radio station calling the play-by-play."

"Naw, I'd have to leave Dancing Deer for a bigger town that actually has a radio station."

"Inez, how tall do you think their Number 1 is? He looks like he might have been Goliath in an earlier age."

"He's probably close to seven feet tall. Tall Paul is six feet five . . . or maybe he's six feet seven. I can never remember. I just know it hurts my neck to look up at him when I'm standing close."

"When have you been close enough to get a neck-ache from looking up at my boyfriend?"

"Every opportunity I get. Besides, he's not your boyfriend yet."

"Yes, he is. I've already decided. It's just that we haven't told anyone."

"Or maybe he's not yet privy to it either."

"One thing at a time, Inez."

"And that's why he's taking you to the homecoming dance instead of Laney."

"That's only a temporary set-back. I've promised to dance with him and, after it's over, he won't ever want to dance with anyone else."

"Sarah, that's exactly the kind of knowledge I need to know. How are you planning on getting it done?"

"I've got all game to figure it out."

"I could help you." Inez waited for Sarah to respond. When nothing was forthcoming she continued with, "Okay. At intermission we get to leave the pep club section to sit with our dates. I don't want Brad to know we're thinking of someone other than him. Just kick me if I get headed in the wrong direction.

"Sarah, look, Paul's talking to Howard. I didn't think they even knew each other. Howard's such a . . . a nobody."

CHAPTER 28—THE GAME BEFORE INTERMISSION
Friday, October 23, 1943

When the time arrived for the game to start Father Donovan O'Reilly walked to the center of the floor in his stocking feet to sing the National Anthem. He had no accompaniment and no amplification. He didn't need either.

Father O'Reilly felt the outline of his harmonica in his pants pocket for luck. He remembered the day he asked his father to teach him to sing. "Donny, the harp is a powerful tool. Use it to set the mood, then follow through with your voice. Together they can quieten children, bring happiness to the elderly, make shy people break out in dance, or bring tears to the strong. If you have patience and give a fair amount of time to practice you can make the men want to be your best friend and the women dream of being your sweetheart."

After becoming a priest, Donovan O'Reilly never used his persuasive musical abilities for personal gain. And he did not need luck for the performance at hand. A week earlier he was given his choice of doing the singing or the praying. He thought about the singing of the other ministers in town and decided to give one of them the opportunity of doing what either one of then was most competent at—which was not singing. Everyone in the gym took off their hats and stood facing the national flag. They crossed their hearts or saluted as they waited. The most wonderful voice in the entire town soon filled the room. Even the people past the double-wide doors, down the hall, standing next to a popcorn popper going crazy punctuating the melody stood stock still, entranced.

Five boys from Dancing Deer faced off in the middle of the hardwood floor against five boys from Skunk Hollow. Tall Paul crouched next to Goliath. The head referee tossed the ball into the air and the Skunk Hollow forward Number 6 broke for their basket. Paul jumped and his hand easily reached the ball several inches higher than his bulkier and slower adversary. Paul slapped the ball to James but, at the last possible moment, the Skunk Hollow guard Number 3 cut in front, caught the ball, and slung it toward the Skunk Hollow goal. The Skunk Hollow forward Number 6, who had broke for the goal at the opening tipoff, grabbed the throw and made an easy layup with no Dancing Deer player within twenty-five feet. Four seconds into the game and Skunk Hollow led two-zip.

James threw the ball in to Steve, who started dribbling toward center court. Two Skunk Hollow forwards fell away from the men they were guarding to help a guard box in Steve. Steve stopped dribbling and was all elbows and arms as he frantically tried to find a place to unload his cargo. Under the goal, a Skunk Hollow guard Number 4 stepped on Paul's foot. Paul pushed him away and the Skunk Hollow player slid and fell backwards. A whistle blew, stopping the action. A black and white striped arm extended Paul's way, awarding him a foul. The ball was given to Skunk Hollow. Paul raised his hand, acknowledging the foul.

Number 3 threw in the ball to Number 4. He dribbled twice and threw to Goliath six feet in front of the basket. Goliath palmed the ball in one hand and held it high overhead. Paul jumped to knock it away, but Goliath tucked it behind his back at the last second. Paul swooshed at an empty spot. Forward Number 5 charged to the goal behind Goliath. The big guy dropped the ball to his team-mate who made an easy layup.

As James brought the ball to Dancing Deer's court, Number 3 rammed an elbow into Paul. Paul shoved him away with Number 3 going limp and falling in front of a referee. A whistle blew, another foul was given to Paul and the ball was again given to Skunk Hollow. Less than a minute into the game and Skunk Hollow was in the lead at four to nothing. Paul had two fouls and Skunk Hollow was driving with the ball.

Inez punched Sarah, "Those Skunk Hollow kids aren't playing fair. Do you see how they foul when the action is on the other side of the court? The referees aren't even looking their way. And when we do something in retaliation those babies fall to the floor. They should be in the movies."

"Oh, Inez. Are you trying to make excuses? It looks to me the Skunk Hollow boys are outplaying our guys."

Goliath stood close to the basket. He caught the ball and casually tossed in another basket. This time James, with the ball, called time and headed to the sidelines with Skunk Hollow ahead by six.

"Okay, guys, what's going on? It looks like those short squirts are faster than Steve or I, and Paul's in foul trouble two minutes into the game." Amos Considine started wringing a towel and pacing back and forth.

Paul said, "I'm being baited. You notice it's not their best player who bumps into me. That's in case he gets caught. If anyone other than their center fouls out, it's no big deal. I got to remain calm and not retaliate."

"Okay, let's get back into this thing," said Amos. He sat down as his team returned to the fray.

By the start of the second period Dancing Deer had started to score and now was behind 36 to 20. Although Paul had been stepped on, kicked, knocked sideways, and had his jersey torn at the neck, he had not garnered any more fouls.

As the game progressed in the second period and with the boys from Skunk Hollow putting a severe beating on the local boys, Inez started showing signs of becoming unstable. "Sarah, it looks to me like the Skunk Hollow boys know what we're about to do before we do it. Sometimes James can't even get the ball thrown in. When John and Andrew run to the basket someone is standing in their route and we get a penalty for charging."

"Inez, what are you talking about? What is charging?"

"I'm not sure, but I think it's when the player with the ball runs over an opponent standing stock still."

"You've already said that."

"Sarah, who is that guy sitting on the front row of the bleachers behind their coach?"

"I have no idea. He's wearing sunglasses and a baseball cap. I don't think he wants anyone to know who he is."

"Well, I've noticed that he sometimes looks through a big book. And, after he does that, he says something to their coach. Sarah! That's Coach Jolly! He's telling their coach what we're going to do next. I got to go." Inez jumped up, stepped over knees, coats, and outstretched hands clasping beverages. She fell over the captain of her row, apologized, and zigzagged to the floor in front of the middle bleachers.

"Mr. Considine, you've got to call timeout. I know why we're losing."

"Calm down, young lady. We're not losing. We're just behind a little bit."

"Mr. Considine, we're behind by 28 points. We got three players in foul trouble, and we're only hitting thirty-five percent of our shots. Call time out. I got to tell Paul what's going on."

"Okay, you seem to know basketball." He looked down at his assistant and said for him to signal to James to take a timeout.

When the players came over to the bench they were hanging their heads. Inez reached through the arms and cups of water to grab Paul by his jersey. "Paul, Coach Jolly has given them your playbook."

"What?"

"There he is sitting right behind their coach. See that book he's carrying?"

"Holy moly."

"Paul, you owe me."

"I do for a fact. What's your name?"

"Inez. I'll save you a dance." Inez turned to go. She was beaming.

"Okay, listen up, guys. Forget all our plays. We're going back out there and play a non-scripted game. I think the easiest way to do that is for James and Steve to change to forwards while Andrew and John do the guard parts. Don't try to remember anything. Just play like we're in the park and have been challenged to a game."

By the end of the second period Dancing Deer had started to climb back into the game. They had whittled the lead down to 22 points. Paul didn't know if there was enough time to win the game, but they'd get it closer in the two remaining periods.

CHAPTER 29—INTERMISSION
Friday, October 23, 1943

Amos Considine led his basketball players off the court and into the hometown locker room. He told Hayden, his assistant, to get a rolling blackboard and chalk while he gathered everyone in a circle. "Gentlemen, we don't have much time, so I propose that we divide these few minutes into two segments. First, Paul will be in charge of planning a strategy against a conniving mob of misfits led by our old coach in disguise. When he's finished, I want to say a few words before we head back out. Paul, show us how we can use this new information to our advantage."

Paul went to the blackboard, placed the chalk against its dark surface, and pulled it back. "I'm sorry, I don't know what we can do." He lowered his hand from the blackboard. "Wait a minute. This is a problem we can work out rationally. Mr. Stout would say to spend most of your efforts on what you do best. If you do that, you won't have time to screw up.

"Okay, so here's what we do. Since they're faster, let's not spend time dribbling, but pass the ball down the court. Let's switch our guards and forwards back to the original lineup. If the ball comes up on the right, Andrew, you go to the center line to help James and Steve. If it comes up on the left, John, you go back. I'll start off at the top of the key and work down to my hook position on the left or jumper on the right. We're down by 22 points so the next two periods will be a shoot-out. When we go back onto the court to get ready for the third period, the shooters should head to the spot where they are most comfortable at making a shot and shoot as many hoops from that single spot as time allows. You second stringers retrieve the balls and feed to the shooters.

"When we're playing defense, don't attack the position they are in, but go to the position where they will be. Don't try to take away the ball from waist-high. Go down and get it inches from the floor. If you get the opportunity, lunge for the ball at where you expect the ball to be. If you're under the basket where the big guy is, keep the ball low. He's

107

awkward and doesn't bend well. Also, don't hold the ball. Receive it and send it. Know ahead of time where your targets will be standing. If you're driving to the target, think about passing off at the last minute. They're working our lanes real well and you're not likely to get through.

"I'll foul out with two more so I won't be charging the basket. I'll be making hooks from ten feet and jump shots from the right or from the top of the key. I hope somebody takes one of the baselines." Paul paused and then placed the chalk in the tray under the rolling blackboard. He said, "We've got to shoot the basket at our first opportunity and we need lots of opportunities. We also need to hit with a high percentage."

"And one more thing. We've got to make our free throws. I know I haven't been good at the line so don't use me as an example." Paul turned toward Mr. Considine, then looking back over his shoulder said, "Steve I'm going to slap the ball on tipoff directly at their bench. John, you go to the basket." Paul raised his hand waist-high with the palm up for Amos Considine.

Amos stood beside his bench. "Gentlemen, as Mr. Stout would say, this is more than a game of basketball. It's a game of what's right prevailing over what's wrong. You can't think that winning by breaking the rules is okay. It's not. Let's do what Paul suggests and play as hard as we can. I don't want any of you to lose your sense of purpose or temper. We are not ballplayers first and gentlemen second. No, we'll win if we can, and if we can't win, we will still hold our heads up because we played by the rules and will not taint our victory or defeat by unsportsmanlike behavior.

"All right, let's go out there and show these upstarts how, like the phoenix rising out of ashes, we will not be denied."

CHAPTER 30—THE GAME AFTER INTERMISSION
Friday, October 23, 1943

The Five Apostles went about their business. After coming out of the locker room each went to the section of the home court he considered his. With the second-stringers feeding balls, the five pumped baskets. From the baseline, Andrew made ten in a row from twenty feet. The only times he missed were when John's ball arrived at the basket at the same time. Paul made several jumpers from the top of the key, then went closer to the basket for his over-the-shoulder hooks.

While the Five Apostles postured for their comeback the Skunk Hollow players slapped each other on the back and kidded around. They thought this game was already won. Coach Jolly threw down the playbook and yanked on the arm of the Skunk Hollow coach. He knew what his old players were capable of and he also knew that if Skunk Hollow didn't play the next two quarters with the same tenacity they had played with before the break, they would find that their school buses had turned into pumpkins and their principal and head coach into two fat rats.

The fans on both sides of the floor watched the Five Apostles. It soon became apparent to everyone in the house—other than the Skunk Hollow Coach and his players—that when the third period started, the Skunk Hollow Polecats had better hold on to their hats and hope they had built up enough of a lead to see them through.

When it was time to play, the Five Apostles walked to their positions like five men with a purpose. The second-stringers rounded up loose balls. Skunk Hollow slowly got into place.

Paul crouched, shot a look at Coach Jolly, and jumped for the ball. He slapped it toward their bench. Steve was there. He smiled at coach Jolly before grabbing the ball and throwing it to John standing under the basket.

grabbed the ball and threw to John standing under the basket. Two points for Dancing Deer. Skunk Hollow brought the ball down court, passed to Goliath and he tossed it in from eight feet.

The second time Dancing Deer got the ball, James threw to an open spot on the back court. Steve was there when the ball arrived. He turned and threw it to half-court where Andrew caught it, dribbled once, and threw to Paul. Paul bounced the ball one time, jumped into the air, and threw a lollipop from twenty-five feet to the basket—nothing but net. The Dancing Deer fans jumped out of their seats, yelling. The Skunk Hollow fans looked down. They knew their boys needed to get serious.

Half-way through the third period the Skunk Hollow players started fouling Paul regularly. Paul could only make twenty percent of his free throws. They had realized that, with their Number 1 under the basket to gather up the re-bound of Paul's missed effort, they had a way to regain the advantage. Their reasoning was necessitated because, if Paul didn't rocket one from ten feet behind the free throw line, Andrew was hitting from somewhere close to Harrison.

"Sarah, the Five Apostles have started taking control. Look how smartly they throw the ball. This is precision. We've still got five minutes in the third period and they've closed to within fifteen points. If Paul could shoot a free throw we'd be even closer."

"I know. Why do you reckon he misses so many of those little easy shots? There isn't anybody pawing at him. He should be making every one."

"Let me think about it. He must be having some mechanical failure. I'd hate to think it was psychological—like it was too easy. I'm going down to talk to him about it."

Brad sat between Sarah and Inez. "How would your mother take it if I told her how to cook biscuits?"

"She'd hit you in the back of your head with a rolling pin."

"So would it be any different for a girl to tell a star basketball player how to hit free-throws?"

"You are so right. What made me think I could be of any help to him. I think I'll go down and tell him what I almost did. Here, Sarah, hold my drink." Inez slowly made her way to Principal Considine. "Sir. Mr. Considine. Why do you think Paul can't make a free throw?"

"I don't know, young lady. Why don't you tell me."

"Fair enough. The arc of the ball is too flat."

"What?"

"Tell him to lob it up there easy. Throw it like a girl with lots of air under it. And if he still can't make a free throw, he needs to toss it to the basket underhanded."

"You want me to tell Tall Paul to throw the ball like a girl?"

"Mr. Considine, what do you have to lose? He's had ten tries this one period and he's made one point. If he doesn't start shooting a better percentage from the free-throw line you'll have to forego the comeback."

"Young lady, step over the bench. Hayden, send them word we want a time out."

Soon the players headed to their respective benches. Amos Considine said, "Fellas, the woman who picked Coach Jolly out of the crowd, the same one who determined he was using our playbook to scuttle our plays, now wants to tell Paul how to make a free throw. Listen up, she might be on to something."

"Paul, your shots are coming in flat. You are so strong you're trying to force the ball through the hoop. You're not thinking about angles. Give me a piece of paper." Hayden, the new assistant coach, handed Inez his notebook. She drew two circles: a flat oval with a wide and skinny center and a completely round one. "Paul, if the basketball had eyes this is what the hoop would look like to the ball the way you're throwing it." Inez held up the picture of the flat oval. "This other one . . ." she held up the round circle "is what it would look like to the ball if you threw like a girl—a ball coming down from a high arc. Lob up the free-throw like I was the one throwing it. And if that still doesn't work, try it underhanded." Inez handed the two drawings to Hayden, then walked around the bench back toward her seat.

John hit Paul on the back and said, "Man, throw it like Inez. Try it."

The Five Apostles went back onto the floor. Hayden walked to the cheerleaders. Inez climbed into her seat beside Brad. "Inez, you are amazing. What did you tell him and what did you write on the paper?"

"Brad, I told him that you was going to slap him silly if he kept missing those easy free-throws. And on the paper I wrote your home address."

"Inez, are you planning on getting me killed?"

"Brad, I didn't say that. I told him I could hit that little basket. He just needed to calm down a little."

James threw in the ball to Steve. Steve turned and threw it to Paul. Paul bounced the ball one time, jumped, and was slammed in the chest by a little guy charging from five feet. The ball sailed over the backboard. The referee called a foul, the little guy proudly raised his hand, and Paul headed to the free-throw line.

Hayden said something to the head cheerleader and she gathered her team. They grabbed their megaphones and yelled, "Throw it like Inez. Throw it like Inez."

Paul bounced the ball once, twice, heard the cheerleaders, and floated up a dying duck. It barely made it to the front rim, took a small bounce, then rolled around to the back and fell in. The crowd were out of their seats, the cheer leaders yelled with increased enthusiasm, and the fans chimed in with, "Throw it like Inez. Throw it like Inez. Throw it like Inez." Paul made his second attempt with ease. The boys from Skunk Hollow took a time-out. They had to come up with an alternative to fouling the Dancing Deer center.

Inez turned red. Brad had yelled louder than anyone in their section. Even Sarah screamed, "Throw it like Inez."

Brad, Sarah, and Inez sat down. Brad said, "Inez, I'll never again doubt anything you ever say. As the Five Apostles are my witnesses, you are a walking miracle."

"Brad, I'm overcome. I'm not sure what it was you just said, but it sounded nice."

The fourth period started with Dancing Deer down by ten points. The score had soared to 85 for Skunk Hollow, 75 for the boys from Dancing Deer.

During the period James stole the ball three times from a fast and sneaky Number 3, Steve got better about bringing the ball past center-court, John and Andrew pumped in their shots from somewhere behind the bleachers, and Paul fouled out with a minute fifteen left to play. Dancing Deer was behind by five. With Tall Paul cooling his heels, Andrew moved to center and Lars came in to play in Andrew's vacated forward position.

The next time they got the ball, James threw the ball in to Steve who threw it to Andrew. Andrew charged the backboard and passed to Lars when his lane closed down. Lars dribbled past the basket from underneath and threw the ball behind him over his head. It hit the backboard and bounded in. Goliath hit Lars' shooting hand as Lars had let it go, sending Lars to the free-throw line for one shot. Lars threw the ball too hard. There was no chance it would go in. When it hit the back of the rim the ball bounced up into the backboard and back to a charging Lars. He caught the ball a foot in front of the basket and plopped it in over Goliath's outstretched arm to bring the score to within one point.

With seven seconds on the clock, Skunk Hollow was ahead by one, and they had the ball. Number 3 threw it in to Number 4, who dribbled in a wide arching circle as the seconds counted down. Steve and James closed in. Number 1 waited close to the basket. Number 4 passed through a tangle of grabbing hands to Number 6. But John stepped in and stole the pass inches from Number 6's face. He quickly tossed to Andrew. The cheerleaders yelled into their megaphones, "Throw it like Inez. Throw it like Inez." From mid-court, Andrew slung the basketball and prayed. The ball soared through the air, the last seconds ticked off the clock, the ball hit the backboard and then the back of the front edge of the rim. It bounded a second time into the backboard. From there it plopped into the center of the basket. The ringer sounded the end of the game. But Dancing Deer had come back—like the phoenix rising from ashes—winning the game 110 to 109. It was the most points ever scored by either team and the first time either team had broken a hundred.

The Dancing Deer fans rushed onto the floor. The Skunk Hollow fans tried to raise the spirits of their gladiators by telling them they were proud of their efforts. The boys from Dancing Deer ran ecstatically around the gymnasium, hugging and lifting anyone coming within reach. John Jolly slinked out the door before someone could come over and yank off his disguise.

That night the school busses from Skunk Hollow made a slow crawl home, much like a funeral procession. The fans from Skunk

Hollow were only a little upset. They saw a wonderful game. They also knew, from the time Paul made his soft free throw, that the game was over. They sat back and enjoyed a marvelous performance from both teams. The fans from Dancing Deer had not been so sure, especially after Tall Paul fouled out. Amos Considine thought he might give up being a principal and become a full-time coach. He'd first have to talk it over with his wife.

CHAPTER 31—THE DANCE
Friday, October 23, 1943

Amos Considine said, "Beth, I'd really like to make an appearance at the dance tonight. Would you mind sashaying around the floor once or twice with me?"

"Amos, you deserve whatever you want. I had no idea you knew so much about basketball. The way you drove your boys to come from so far behind. The manner in which you picked apart their strategy to give Dancing Deer a fighting chance. I'm so proud I could bust."

"Actually, Beth, honey, I don't know much about basketball. Most of what I was able to do was to stand back and watch five—no, better make that six—wonderful young men reach into their storehouse of abilities and fashion something that worked. I better add Inez into the cauldron because without her . . . without Inez, we would not have won."

"You're just downplaying the role you played."

"No. My best work was putting us in a position where someone else could step up and say, 'I can get us there from here.'"

I handled the irate mothers, allowed coach Jolly to abandon ship, and play-acted being a basketball coach. My only failing was not being able to work things out with Mr. Stout."

"Darling, let's not dwell on the failures, but enjoy the successes. Will there be many of those new-fangled dances?"

"Yo, Inez. Good game, girl."

"I thought so."

"You happen to have any open slots on your dance card?"

"I might." Inez watched as a slender, brunette classmate swung a purse at her talkative date and stormed off down the hall. The date was trying his best to catch up and offering a multitude of apologies.

Brad turned to one of his two dates. "Inez, who was that guy?"

"Beats me."

Sarah had her arm through Brad's. "Inez, the way people are staring at you we better go to the powder room first chance we get. You might be missing an article of clothing."

"Nonsense. Besides, I like it."

"Brad, do you think we could get a table closer to the dance floor?" asked Sarah.

"Sarah, come on. Let's drag Brad. Surely one of those tables will have three empty seats."

A lanky boy with pale blond hair approached Inez. "My date and I have a table down front would you care to join us?"

"There's three. And, we'll need a fourth that'll be vacant for a while."

"Actually we got more than one table. Having four empty seats together is no problem at all."

Sarah, Brad, and Inez followed the lanky boy toward the stage. "Make way, everybody, I got Inez."

Paul walked out of the boys locker room and noticed a man wearing a suit, leaning against a tiled wall. As Paul approached, the man held out his hand. "Dale Duggan, University of Arkansas."

"Pleased to meet you, Mr. Duggan. You come all the way from Fayetteville to watch our game?"

"I did and I am certainly glad I did. Son, you played a marvelous game. Have you given any consideration to college after you graduate?"

"Some."

"Well, let me tell you about the advantages of going to the University of Arkansas. We're the biggest in the state. While other teams play all over the great state of Arkansas and others close by, we play our games all over the south. There's going to be other colleges knocking on your door, but I hope you'll put ours at the top of your list. I think I can even help you with a scholarship."

"I'd like to take a tour of the campus first."

"Here. Take my card. Talk it over with your parents and give me a call. You let me know when you can come up. I'll send you bus tickets and meet you at the station. Your parents too. Everything paid by the university of course."

116

"You offer degrees in philosophy?"

"We do, but you might be the first basketball player ever to want one. When you come up I'll take you to their building and introduce you to Dean Jacobson, the head of the department."

"That sounds great, Mr. Duggan."

"So, Paul. Do you think Andrew might be interested?"

Paul shook Mr. Duggan's hand and walked to where Laney waited. When he got there her two friends and their dates were also there. Paul held out his arm and said, "Laney, you look so pretty. Would you care to join me for a little get-together we have planned in your honor?"

"It would be my pleasure, Paul." Laney took Paul's arm and the two of them led the group down the hall to the cafeteria.

When they walked through the doors, the crowd opened up a broad walkway to the center table. A bouquet of flowers sat in the middle. Paul pulled out a chair for Laney and waited for her attendants to be seated before he sat down.

"Paul, that was a wonderful game. How did you figure out how to fight back? At one time they had you down by thirty points."

"It wasn't me. It was Inez. She's the one who figured it out and she also figured out why I wasn't making my free-throws."

In the background, the band played. The people milling around socializing found their seats and waited for the homecoming queen and her escort to open up the dance floor. Paul and Laney embraced and danced in circles to the music. About halfway through the dance, her two attendants and their escorts joined them. After the dance Paul took Laney back to their table. Before he could sit down, Howard walked up and tapped him on the shoulder. Paul turned and shook hands with Howard. He leaned in to Laney.

"I've been talking to Howard. He tells me you are actually his date. After listening to his story I have to agree. So, Laney, this is where I leave you. Howard will see you home. No one need know the circumstances. Don't call me or let anyone think you're my girlfriend. Goodbye, Laney." Paul turned and left for a glass of punch.

After two more dances the students were into the swing of things. The band belted out the currently popular songs. And Sarah had danced one time with Brad. Paul walked up to their table and asked Inez if she would like to dance. Inez was overcome with joy.

As they made it to the floor Inez noticed there were not as many dancers as before and some left as she and Paul entered. Then a spotlight, operated by a technical savvy Hayden, illuminated the couple. Inez looked around. The floor was empty. Her eyes wandered the room and noticed that the basketball players had ringed the dance floor. With the band playing a slow waltz she and Paul glided from one end of the floor to the other. It was her greatest moment.

After the dance, the basketball players allowed other dancers on as Paul and Inez walked off. When Paul pulled her chair out, James walked up and asked if he might have the next dance. Paul pushed her chair back under the table and sat in the empty seat to the right of Sarah. Paul nodded to the lanky boy sitting across the table. He said, "Thank you, Lars."

"My pleasure."

Brad sat on the other side of Sarah. He leaned forward and said, "How did you do it, Paul? The way the game started everyone thought it would be a blowout."

"It would have been had Inez not figured things out."

"I know. The girl's a marvel. Do you really think that was coach Jolly behind their bench?"

"Yeah. He's a regular Benedict Arnold."

When the band started a new song Brad asked Sarah if she would like to dance "Not right now, Brad. I'm waiting for Inez to return. She's danced four times in a row, and all with basketball players. Twice with James."

"I know. She's raced ahead right out of my league."

Paul twirled his glass of punch. "Don't be so hard on yourself, Brad. Inez is up in the clouds right now. But you're what she'll see when she takes off those rose-colored glasses. A girl has to dream. But someone solid, a person fun to be around, someone she feels comfortable with, someone that can be counted on in the clutch, that's a person to be cherished. A companion like that enters into a relationship with a sense of worth that exceeds anything fleeting no matter how exhilarating for the moment."

"Paul, I'd always taken you as someone—well, not so blooming deep. You're now sounding like Mr. Stout."

"And that's not a bad thing, is it?"

Sarah took Paul's hand saying, "Not a bad thing at all."

"Sarah, would you dance with me?"

"Yes. I will. It looks like Inez is going to stay out there a while longer."

Paul followed Sarah to the floor. "I'm not much of a dancer—mostly legs and arms flailing about to some internal kinetic kettle-drumming."

"Paul, where do you come up with those evocative words? Are you planning on being a writer?"

"That would be interesting. But I don't think I could be creative enough or have the required breadth of imagination. Still, I might try my hand at it someday. Right now I'm trying to think up some way to make this dance memorable—a crackerjack. So I won't have to wait till Doomsday for a second effort."

"Mr. Mitchell, you don't have to worry about that. I've decided to give you as many dances as you can handle, as often as you want."

Paul stopped dancing. He placed a hand on each side of Sarah's face and kissed her. It was a passionate kiss, first on her lower lip then moving up slowly caressing the curve of half a smile. With his teeth he nibbled. His right hand moved to Sarah's neck. She murmured. Her knees buckled and Paul had to hold tight to keep her from sliding through his embrace. He kissed her upper lip and tugged on it as he held it tight between his tongue and upper lip. Sarah thought she might faint and beat on Paul's shoulder.

Paul backed away and twirled Sarah in a circle as the song ended. Sarah had to get her breath back. She said, "Paul Mitchell, you better not let my dad see you kiss me that way. He'd be after a shotgun."

"Would that be so bad?"

"Not in the least." Sarah took Paul's hand and staggered back to their table. On the way she said to no one in particular, "I'll never be the same."

Sarah sat in her chair and used the "Reserved" table sign to fan her face. Inez arrived at the table on the arm of Andrew. She said, "Sarah, let's go to the powder room I've got to get my breath back."

"Me too."

On the way, Inez told Sarah what a wonderful time she was having and how the boys were so attentive. She looked back over her shoulder and said, "Right now they're shoving tables together so we can sit as one big group."

"Inez, what about Brad? I think he's beginning to feel left out. Do you remember how that felt?"

"Yes, I do. When we get back I'll ask him to dance. And if you would ask his opinion on something and I'll get James, Andrew, and Steve to include him in their conversations."

"Inez, do you remember us talking about your desire to solve everyone's problems?"

"Yes."

"Then just act normal and sit beside him and I'll be on the other side. After all, he's our date."

"Oh, Sarah, I'm having the best time."

"Me, too."

Back at the table, Paul asked Brad why he didn't try out for the basketball team.

"I've always been too clumsy. My friends chide me about it all the time. So, I guess, the reason is that I thought I wasn't good enough."

"Why don't you show up on Monday and I'll give you some pointers."

James said, "Yeah, it takes people with different abilities to make up a team. Steve and I are not that good at shooting baskets so we work on dribbling and bringing the ball up the court. If you want I could show you the routines we use to hone that skill. What about baseball? You going to try out for the baseball team?"

Andrew said, "What you need to do is to have me or Steve help you decide what position you're best suited for and then, for that one position, learn everything you can. It's much easier if you stick to one from the start. Most of us played everything before we found the position we liked the best. You got a glove?" A few minutes later Andrew left for refreshments.

The two girls returned from the ladies room to find the conversation had migrated away from them to Brad. Inez leaned over and said, "Brad, would you dance with me?"

Sarah had her shoe off and rubbed her foot against Paul's leg. Several people came by to tell Paul what a good game he played. One man said, "Paul, you ought to think about coaching."

"No. My future is all set. The University of Arkansas has offered me a scholarship to play for them. I plan to take them up on the offer, get a degree in philosophy, and come back here to run my family's ranch."

"How is getting a degree in philosophy going to help you run your ranch?"

"It won't. Getting a degree in philosophy is going to help me run my life."

Andrew returned from the refreshment bar with a tray of drinks. As he passed them around he said to Paul, "You talk to that guy from Fayetteville?"

"Yeah. I'm going to be a razorback."

"Then I will as well. You and me, Paul."

Sarah put her hand on Paul's. She looked into his eyes and said, "You and me, Paul."

PART II
THE PRIEST

CHAPTER 32—DONOVAN O'REILLY
Cloonfad, Ireland, March 1907

"Come along, Donny. We have to get back before the rain gets here. See how black the sky is."

Donovan O'Reilly's father was a kind man. He rarely yelled at Donny or his mother. Lately though, Donny knew something was amiss. Tension was in the air. No kidding like usual. No good-natured pats on the back or gentle shove in an effort to speed him up when he wanted to stop and look at something, to stomp his foot in a water puddle. Donny was keenly aware something was not quite right.

"Dad, do you think Grandpa will be okay?"

"I don't know. He's had one of these spells before. The doctor says there's nothing he can do. We'll have to have a family meeting and decide what's best." Donny's father reached over a hand and adjusted the bill of Donny's cap. "Son, let's run the rest of the way. It's not far. What do you say?"

"I say that the last one there has to dry the dishes." Donny immediately started in a full run to the small cottage at the top of the next hill.

Right before Donny reached the door, an elderly woman pulled it open and hugged the exhausted boy. Next came her eldest son and after letting go of the boy she took her son's coat and hat. "What did he say?"

"Mom, Dad's not going to be able to work in the fields any more. The doctor said his heart wouldn't hold out. The rest of us will have to pick up the slack and let him supervise from a comfortable chair."

"Terry, we need to make a plan. After the evening meal let's talk about it. Your brother worked on the roof all day. He's asleep in the front room. We'll all decide what's best."

The old man came in from the bedroom on the west side of the house and sat down at the table. Everyone was there: his two boys, the wife and child of his oldest boy, and his wife, his life's companion. "Terry, did he give you any pills?"

"Yes. He gave me two bottles. But he took hold of my arm and said if you didn't take it easy he wanted one bottle back because you wouldn't be with us long enough to start using it."

"That doctor. He always did have a sense of humor."

After everyone sat down, Terry's mother thanked the Good Lord for giving them another day and providing them with another meal. She also said a silent prayer that whatever decision they made that night would be the right one.

After the meal and after Terry's mother had cleaned off the table and her daughter-in-law Maude had washed the dishes for Terry to dry, everyone went into the front room.

Terry said, "If it's all right I'll begin by stating what everyone already knows. This farm does not produce enough crops to pay the rent to Lord Chaney and have enough left to feed the entire family. We don't have enough land and he's not willing to rent us any more. And, since he and the other land owners control the prices they pay for our crops, more land is not the answer anyway."

Loren, Terry's kid brother, said, "I agree, but what we need is a bigger garden."

"You might be right, but I'm thinking me and Maude should take Donny and move into town. I could find a job in one of the stores or offices and we'd be all right. Then you could reduce the amount of land under cultivation and give the sheep more pasture. It would mean a lot less work for you. And, I think, the sheep would be more productive and generate more income for the amount of effort required. With fewer mouths to feed, the three of you should be just fine.

Looking directly at Loren, Terry continued with, "With Mom taking care of the chickens and the three goats, your time would be spent raising potatoes on that fertile area down by the river and barley on the big field on Toke Hill. Every thing else could be turned over to the sheep. The dogs do all of the work. All Dad would have to do is— nothing. Absolutely nothing."

"Now see here. I'm not going to sit around the house all day. Don't you think I could follow the dogs as they take out the sheep?"

"If you feel like it."

Loren spoke up again. "Terry, that sounds good except there aren't any jobs in town. No one has any work at all. That's why our prices are so low. No one has any money to buy our crops, so we have to take what Lord Chaney and his friends offer."

"Well, I've heard that the railroad is building a spur from Claremorris to Ballinrobe. They'll need workers. I've already talked it over with Maude. Tomorrow I'm going to Claremorris to see when the work starts and look for us a cheap place to stay. We'll move as soon as I get paid a couple of times."

The next morning Terry O'Reilly took a parcel of food his mother had prepared and started the eighteen-mile hike to Claremorris. He felt pretty good about the family meeting. It was always good to work from a plan. If the plan was well thought out, if allowances were made for all possible contingencies, and if the starting spot was within a person's grasp, all one had to do was stick to the plan.

Terry entered Claremorris in the early afternoon and went straight to the train station. Several people milled around with clipboards. He confidently walked inside the stationhouse to the station master's office. After knocking on the door, a young lady pushed a glass panel to one side in a wooden trough. She stuck her head out and told Terry, who was still standing by the door, "Come over here."

"Good day, Miss."

"Tickets are sold outside. Go back through the front door and the ticket window is on your right." She started to slide the glass panel back into place.

"Uh . . . no. I want to help build the spur to Ballinrode."

"We've got all the workers we need. Filled the quota two hours after posting."

"You got any skilled positions?"

"Yeah. We got a few of those. You ever work with explosives?"

"No."

"You an engineer?"

"No. But I can work with rock. You'll need masons for the overpasses, bridges, and stationhouse."

"Here. Fill this form out and be here Monday morning at six. Bring your lunch and the form back with you."

"How much will I make?"

"Whatever the going rate is. And you need to be plenty thankful you got a job."

CHAPTER 33—FIRST DAY ON THE JOB
Claremorris, Ireland, March 1907

Terry O'Reilly spent the night on a bed of rushes he had gathered and piled on an isolated creek bank. Before daylight he bathed in the cool flowing water of a small stream and, putting his things in a canvas bag, headed into town. Terry arrived at the Claremorris train station just as dawn broke. A yard full of happy workers had gathered in tiny circles of two to five people. Most held slips of paper and wore light jackets as the temperature was not expected to get above fifty. It was a glorious day to be working on the railroad—or just to be working at all.

A man walked from the stationhouse saying, "Let's have those papers."

The rest of the day Terry worked as a common laborer. He was glad for it though because nothing was ready for masonry work and he had expected the boss to tell him his services were not yet needed, to check back in a week or so when it would be time to construct the first overpass or bridge or whatever needed concrete or rock work.

One group of men started putting down railroad ties as soon as a bulldozer had prepared the ground with packed gravel. A second group of men were told to drain a bog at Curramore and to head in that direction on the back of a flat-bed truck. A third group of men rode on the back of a second flat-bed truck to the site of the first overpass. After jumping down from the truck, each was handed a shovel or a pickax. As soon as the man in charge had marked the area, they prepared the ground for concrete pillars. Terry was with the men on this second truck.

On the drive from the railroad station he learned that most of the workers would be saving their paychecks for steerage tickets to America where a worker is appreciated, jobs are plentiful, the wages in line with the work performed, and land is available for anyone to purchase. From the conversations he overheard, Terry confirmed his belief that America was as close to paradise as someone still kicking was likely to find.

129

Other people from his town of Cloonfad had emigrated and sent letters to those who stayed behind. Usually money was enclosed, adding to the mystique accompanying their emigration. Sometimes along with the money was a ticket for passage.

Of course not everyone from Ireland left for America. Some went to Canada, Australia, New Zealand, or South America. No one from Cloonfad had left for South America. Gaelic was the traditional language of Ireland, but English had moved up and eventually overtaken it as the predominant tongue. But going to South America required the emigrant learn a new language: Spanish for most countries and Portuguese for Brazil. For Terry, if he and his family emigrated, it would be to America—the land of plenty.

To the man swinging a pickax next in line, Terry asked, "How long do you suppose the work will hold out?"

"A couple of years or more. I worked on a similar spur out of Limerick and it took us that long. The pay's good, but I couldn't bring my family. Would have used up all my earnings to pay for their food and lodging."

"But you had to pay for your food and lodging. Couldn't you have squeezed in your wife and a kid or two?"

"No. Several of us rented a room together. To keep it as cheap as possible we slept together dormitory style. We've done the same here. You interested in joining us? We got room for one more."

"Yeah. But I can't pay until I get my first wages."

"That's okay. Smiley is good with figures. He'll add you and let you know how much is your share. It'll be a bit more for you next month and a little less for us because the rest of us paid your share to the end of this month. After that first payment, Smiley will recalculate and everyone will pay the same amount."

"You going to America?" Terry sat on the edge of the truck bed and swayed with each turn. The truck bed contained a pile of gravel in the middle with the men sitting cross-legged around it. One man fell off when a rear wheel hit a hole in the road. They yelled at the driver, but he kept the truck moving. The unlucky worker had to hike the rest of the way to the work-site.

"Yeah. Had enough money the first go-round but got into a card game and lost it all. I had to sleep with one eye open for a month."

"With one eye open?"

The man continued, "I was afraid of what my wife might do to me if she thought I was deep in sleep."

CHAPTER 34—SAYING GOODBYE
Roscommon, Ireland, April 1909

For the next two years Terry O'Reilly worked for the Westport Balling-Dublin Railway. He saved every penny he was paid, using only a small portion to pay for his tiny space in the communal room he shared with seven other workers and another portion for the meager amounts of food he consumed.

Early on, Terry had decided he and his family needed to leave the Emerald Isle for a new beginning in the new world. Neither Terry nor anybody in Terry's family had traveled much. One time when he was a child, Terry's father took him south to Blarney Castle to cure his hesitancy to talk. And when he was still a young man barely past puberty, Terry's father took him to Dublin for the funeral of a relative. Except for those two times Terry had not been out of County Mayo or County Roscommon and Donny had not been farther than his hometown of Cloonfad. Maude had moved from the town of Roscommon to Cloonfad when she and Terry married. She also had only been in those same two counties: Roscommon and Mayo. All three were giddy with anticipation for the magical adventure awaiting them.

As the next two years proceeded, Maude went from thinking the trip to America was pie in the sky to thinking they might actually leave Ireland. Her mood shifted from elation for the adventure to worry of not knowing what to expect; from pride in her husband as he put his family first and worked hard to provide to anger with him for taking her away from the family, the community, and the country she loved. As Terry completed his work for the railroad, Maude planned a trip to see her parents. It might be the last time she would see them.

She had not quite figured out how she was going to make the trip when Loren announced he would be going to Dublin with Rob Matthews. Someone had bought one of Rob's dogs and they were delivering it. Rob Matthews was a breeder and trainer of border collies and was known throughout Ireland for the quality of his animals.

"Loren, might Donny and I go as far as Roscommon? We could ride in the back and be no trouble."

"Sure. I better ask Rob first, but I'm certain he won't mind. We'll be staying two nights in Dublin, so you have time for a nice visit."

When Rob arrived in his truck the dog sat in the cab. Loren said, "Maude, he treats his dogs like they're people. If you don't mind a little dog-slobber you're welcome to sit in the cab and let two of the men in your family have the back. I promise to keep Donny from flying out. That way your hair won't blow."

"Let me look at the dog." Maude walked to the truck and thanked Rob for allowing her and her son to tag along. She returned to Loren. "The dog seems well-mannered and really just a puppy, but I think you had better ride up front. Mr. Matthews and I wouldn't have anything to talk about and he's your friend. He asked you, not me. I would feel more comfortable in the back. Besides it's just forty miles."

Maude's family had always been shopkeepers and in their store was where she and Terry had first met. Her dad had not been feeling well, so Maude managed the store while he was plied with home-made remedies by a loving wife. Maude had helped before, but when Terry O'Reilly walked in on his trip to Dublin, she found her tongue was glued to the back of her throat, a wart had mysteriously appeared on her nose, and all her fingers had turned to thumbs. Terry was the handsomest man she had ever met. He had short curly hair, a strong chin, and a sharp-pointed nose chiseled out of a smiling face. But what made him handsome was the way he carried himself and the melodious sound that filled the room when he talked.

"Miss, I need a new axel pin and a pint of grease." The words effortlessly rolled over his tongue as if he were singing. Maude couldn't answer. She couldn't move. Her head was filled with wild fantasies as she stared at a smiling man with a twinkle in his eye.

"Uh . . ." Maude coughed then stammered. "I know—I know where the grease is, but—but you'll have to give me a minute to locate the axel pin." She kicked the ladder then grabbed it as it began scooting away on rollers down a metal track. She then pushed the ladder to the area she thought might contain the axel pins. When she placed her foot on the first step, it slid through and she was stuck. Trying to adjust her shoe she found she could not retract it without turning her foot sideways. Reaching through to remove her shoe she said, "Do you know the diameter of the wheel?"

"No. But I think the pins are all the same."

"You sure? Do you have the broken one with you?" Maude dropped her pencil while ascending the ladder and almost fell off in a vain attempt to catch it.

"No. Lost it." The young man bent to pick up the pencil then steadied the ladder as Maude took a few more steps up.

"And the cart?"

"A few miles out of town. Guarded by my father and a small, feisty dog."

Maude descended the ladder with a cardboard box in her hand. "Okay. Here are the pins, but there are four different sizes. Did you measure the hole it will fit in?" She dropped the box onto the counter and two of the pins flew out, hit the floor, and sailed under an adjacent counter.

"No. And I don't have enough money to buy but the one so how about I take all four, fix the cart, pay for the one I use, and give you back the other three?" The nice-looking man squatted low to the floor and began looking for the two wayward pins.

Maude got down on her knees behind the counter and reached a hand under, "Could you leave me something of value so I can be sure you'll return?"

Terry pulled out something from under the front of the counter enveloped in cobwebs. It looked like a gear-puller. He crawled along the counter with his hand feeling for the two lost pins, "What would you like?"

Maude found one of the pins then came to the end of the counter. She looked directly into the face of her customer. "Your shoes."

Terry held the second of the two lost pins. "Miss, I'd have blisters after walking that far without shoes. How about my hat?" He stood up.

Maude got to her feet as well. "No, that won't do. Check your pockets and see what else you've got."

"I don't have anything in my pockets other than my harmonica and I never let it out of my sight. Other than that—just this dab of money my father sent me into town with to buy the two items."

"Then, I'll lock the door and walk to the cart with you. You can bring me back after you've fixed it."

"Miss, nothing much scares you does it?"

"No."

"And no one is going to say anything about you and I together without a proper chaperone?"

"You might have something there. Just stay right here." Maude looked for her mother and told her to bring a parasol. A nice man wanted to take them for a walk.

Terry and Maude wrote letters for the next four years with Terry coming to Roscommon every holiday. When he was old enough, he came and whisked her away.

Winding through the narrow streets of Roscommon, Rob Matthews drove past the Roscommon *Gaol*. Maude put her hand on Donny's shoulder and said, "That window is famous." She pointed to a window on the third floor.

"A long time ago a woman, called Lady Betty, moved here with a son after her husband died. She was a literate woman who had taught her son to read and write. She also told him that money could buy happiness and without it life was miserable." Donny adjusted his position so he could see the *gaol* better. He had never traveled anywhere before and a story made any place more memorable.

"The son eventually grew up and left her and Ireland by sailing to America. Then one dark and stormy night, many years later, a nicely dressed man in a full beard appeared at her door asking for a meal and a room for the night. She was in the habit of letting out her spare room for extra money and had told several people to steer her way anyone seeking shelter if they looked like they could afford to pay. She asked the man in and through some casual questioning found that no one in town knew he had come to her house. During the wee hours of the morning she crept into his room and killed him. Then, while going through his coat pockets, she discovered he was her son. She became hysterical and ran into the street yelling what she had done."

136

Donny leaned forward so he would not miss any of the story. This was where his mother had grown up and was looking forward to getting a glimpse of what her life had been like when she was his age. "Was this when you were a kid?"

"No, Donny. This was long before I had been born." Maude knew she was not as good a storyteller as Terry—still, Donny was hanging on every word. "At the trial she was found guilty and sentenced to hang. When the time came, she was thrown in a prison cart with several other condemned criminals and hauled through the streets and a heckling crowd to the scaffold. The executioner was either sick or had some other excuse for not showing and the sheriff worried that he would have to do the nasty business himself. Realizing his apprehension, Lady Betty stood up and shouted that if she would be pardoned, she'd hang the lot."

"A woman executioner?"

"Yes. Women can do more than cook and wash and clean house. But let me continue. The sheriff took her aside and they reached a compromise. During the next two hours she hanged everyone in the cart. The sheriff had her sentence commuted and she lived for thirty years in a room on the third floor of the *gaol*.

"She braided and tied her own ropes and had a lapboard attached with a hinge to the windowsill. A rope hung from a pin outside, above the window and, when it was time for her to perform her grisly duty, she placed a noose over their heads and had the condemned step up onto her windowsill and walk out the opening on the lapboard with their hands tied behind their backs. She then tripped a lever next to the window. The lapboard swung down on the hinge and fell against the side of the building. The prisoners kicked and flailed with their legs. While they were dying, she sat in a chair on the other side of the window and sketched their picture."

"Mom, how does hanging kill someone?"

"Sometimes the knot on the noose holds their head at an angle and when they pull up abruptly at the end of a short fall their neck breaks. If that doesn't happen then their throat gets crushed and they suffocate." Maude shivered, thinking about the last few minutes for a hanged person. "When Lady Betty passed away they found pictures of the people she had killed attached to the walls of her room. Now people swear they see her at night peering out that window."

"Mom, that's scary. Have they got those pictures somewhere? Could we see them? Will they let us go inside the *gaol* to see her room?"

"Donny, I thought you said it was scary."

"Yeah, but not to me. I'm going to be a priest someday and dealing with death is just something I'll help people with."

"A priest? Really?"

CHAPTER 35—A PINT OF GUINNESS
Cloonfad, Ireland, May 1909

On Saturday nights after six weary days of work and six weary nights of sleeping in a room with seven snorting diesels, Terry gladly walked the eighteen miles home to sleep in his own bed next to his wife. Donny slept on a pallet in his grandparents' room when his dad was home so his parents could have some privacy. Donny didn't understand the privacy bit. He slept in the same room as his parents before his dad started working on the railroad and couldn't understand why he had to go to the western bedroom the one night each week when his dad came home.

One Sunday Donny feigned sickness and was allowed to sleep with his dad while everyone else attended Mass at the Catholic Church. "Dad, why don't we get the western bedroom? It's larger than this one and that way I could stay with you and Mom."

"Because, Donny, we Irish have always believed that the land of the dead lay in the mythical isles of the west. When people travel that direction they seldom come back. More often than not those same people die young. So your grandparents have the western bedroom, as that is the direction they will eventually travel. They've lived long lives, with hardship and toil every step of the way and will welcome being taken into the bosom of our dear Lord and Savior, whether he requires them to travel west or not."

"Which direction is America?"

"It's west and everyone will come here bringing food for a big meal the night before we leave. It's a wake for us because probably no one here will ever see us again. Some people call it a departure feast, but I like the traditional term 'wake .'"

Donny didn't know what to think. He looked forward to riding on the train and on the ship, but he hadn't thought about never seeing his grandparents again. And there was Uncle Loren. "Will we be able to take my dog?"

"No, Donny. Sam's a working dog. Your grandpa needs Sam to help take care of the sheep."

"Dad, if I work really hard with Uncle Loren and don't eat much, could we stay?"

"Ha, ha. Son, you make me proud. But we're going so that you can grow up big and strong and have your own family and your own land and always have plenty of food for your family. And that can't be done nowadays in dear old Ireland."

"How much longer before we leave?"

"Just another month or so. We're building the stationhouse right now. That's the last bit of work they have for me."

"Will we have enough money?"

"Yes, I think so. We can't be wasteful, but I think we'll have enough to get us there and eat for a few weeks until I find a job."

"But not enough to take anyone else?"

"No. But if someone else wanted to come I could send them a ticket after I got a job."

"Whew, that's great. Let's send three tickets so everyone can come."

"Okay, I'll put you in charge of talking them into it."

A month later Terry returned with his final pay and said it was time to pack their things and say their goodbyes. Maude said they didn't have much to pack, but saying the goodbyes might take a day or two. The next morning everyone went into town. Grandpa needed a new whetstone, Loren wanted to buy some screening and staples, Maude wanted a suitcase for their clothes, and Donny planned on asking for a yo-yo. He had never asked for anything before and felt sick at his stomach when he approached his dad with the request. Donny's grandmother was going simply because she didn't want to stay home while everyone else went to town. Besides, someone had to coordinate the wake.

While the men went one direction, Maude and Grandmother O'Reilly went another with instructions to buy a red yo-yo for Donny. After making their purchases, the men went into the Rude Rooster for a glass of stout. Grandpa and Loren knew they might never see Terry and

Donny again. They needed this male bonding before saying a final farewell. The four O'Reillys sat at a table by the front window so they could see when the women had finished and would be looking for their men.

Terry said, "Loren, have you thought about getting married?"

"Some. When you and Maude got married I thought I wouldn't be able to as that would bring more mouths to the table than our farm could feed. But now that the three of you are heading to America, Mom might appreciate some help in the kitchen. Our flock of sheep is the largest we've ever had so—yes, I have considered getting married."

Grandpa took a big swig and put his tankard on the table. "You need any help picking one out?"

"You got someone in mind, Dad?"

"Not yet, but I'll start looking. I always thought Maude had a lot of spunk but was too skinny. I like my women with more meat on the bone. And big breasted. Yep. Them's two features I can admire in a woman."

Terry looked at his father. "What about a woman with a hefty dowry? Would that be important to you?"

"Nope. Just a hefty one on the left and a hefty one on the right."

"Any other particular quality other than size?"

"Yep. I would prefer that they could stand on their own."

Loren shook his head. "Dad, are we talking about a wife for me or a dancer for the Rude Rooster?"

Donny saw his mother come out of a store and look in both directions. "They're ready to go. There's Mom and . . . and there comes Grandma right now."

Terry said, "All right. let's finish the Guinness and take 'em home."

Grandpa said, "I want to see the dancers."

"There aren't any dancers, Dad. I was just being funny. Why don't you make me a list of the women you think I should consider and I'll start interviewing."

141

CHAPTER 36—THE WAKE
Cloonfad, Ireland, May 1909

When the day came for final goodbyes, people arrived in the late afternoon with pots of food. Tables were set up and the food spread out. Terry had purchased three cases of Guinness and several of the men brought more. While the women congregated in the cooking area, the men sat on the edge of the porch, tree stumps, chairs if any were handy, and the fence separating Donny's play area from the working farm. Each man held a bottle and each man told a story. Donny had the best time of his life. Many years later he would retell these stories when attending dull parties needing more energy.

When Loren brought out his father's list of potential wives, the men gave their opinions. Some had daughters of their own and couldn't understand why a few made the list and others did not. Grandpa got a little red in the face when one man figured out the common feature of each girl on the list.

Another man said they ought to have a contest with marriage to Loren as the prize. The man said, "Son, if you do this right, you could make enough money to keep yourself in Guinness for many a year."

"How's that?"

"Well, you'll need help deciding on the best one. You could charge any man who wanted to help in the judging. You see, a lot of physical characteristics would have to be observed and compared one woman to another. We'd have to look for false advertising, blemishes, hip displacement, and . . ."

"Whoa, we all know what you're talking about when you say false advertising and, of course, blemishes would require a close inspection of a woman all over her body, but what is this 'hip displacement?'"

"You know how some cows have an easy time birthing and some not so easy. It's the same with women. One with wide hips will spit out a kid with hardly any effort, but a woman with narrow hips will have a difficult time and cost a man a lot of money."

"I'm a breast man myself. I wouldn't mind giving up the wide hips for a nice set of jugs." Loren and Terry didn't have to see the speaker to recognize the voice. Terry put his head in his hands.

Loren spoke up, "Maybe we could make it into a four or five-round match. We ask every woman in town who's single, or any woman who planned on being single when I was ready, to enter the contest. We'd have—like five judges picking out the best twenty candidates. A second set of judges would be assembled, with a higher ante, to whittle it down to seven. At that point we'd have to get real personal. I'd want to see up close and in action what I was going to have to share a bed with. Of course, the judges would have to see as well in order to get down to the final three. To determine the one chosen from those three would take weeks and efforts from several different positions. Many separate wifely aspects would be fully investigated. In this instance the three judges would be with me every step of the way. I'd listen to their comments, but, the final choice would have to be mine."

One man said, "I'd pay to be one of those judges." The man tossed his empty bottle of Guinness and grabbed another.

"Me, too."

A third man said, "Comparing the naked torsos of all the single women in our area holds a lot of interest for me. I'd pay dearly for the opportunity. But if I was the man choosing, I'd want to taste her cooking, see how fast she could bake a loaf of bread, and compare her preserves for clarity, sweetness, and texture. I think I'd also pay just to help come up with the areas of interest we'd be looking at."

"Yeah, and how strong she was. I mean, will it take her all day to bring up two buckets of water from the well? And can she cut her own firewood? Hand me another bottle."

"Well, living with one woman for the rest of your life requires more than her being beautiful, a good cook, and a hard worker. I'd want someone who could entertain me."

"You mean like dancing around a pole?"

"No. I mean like making up a limerick."

"Yeah, that's good. Somebody pass me down a bottle."

When the women said it was time to eat, the men walked a little crookedly into the serving area carefully scrutinizing each woman passed. The women felt ill at ease from the stares and wondered what the men had been talking about.

For two hours after the meal, a lot of eyes were dabbed with linen handkerchiefs. Donny, Maude, and Terry were hugged by every woman there. Donny said later that some women took advantage of the opportunity and hugged him more than once. Maude took several messages to deliver to loved ones who had already emigrated to America. She was also given sealed letters with poorly constructed addresses and small amounts of money for postage.

At ten, one man opened a case to retrieve a fiddle and a second brought out a melodeon. Maude brushed against Terry and, with an arm on his shoulder, whispered, "The women want you to sing Danny Boy."

By twelve the women had all the hugging, crying, frivolity, and dancing they could tolerate. They said their final goodbyes and headed home. The men headed into town for more Guinness.

CHAPTER 37—LEAVING HOME
Cloonfad, Ireland, May 1909

At four o'clock in the morning after the wake, Terry lightly shook his wife and said, "Honey, it's time to leave."

An hour later Terry, Maude, and Donny said goodbye and left three teary-eyed relatives on the front porch. Terry carried the suitcase, Maude had the stack of letters and notes given her the previous evening, and Donny clutched a yo-yo in his pocket.

It was eighteen miles to the train station in Claremorris and they had to be there in time to buy tickets and board by nine. There was a later departure at three in the afternoon, but the train leaving at nine got them into Queenstown at a decent time to rent a room for the night. Terry hoped they would not have to wait many days for a ship. The less money spent on this end meant more on the other.

Donny rubbed the sleep from his eyes and worked hard not to slow their pace. No other travelers walked on the lane. The moon's pale light reflecting flecks of grey from the granite rocks strewn from edge to edge made Donny shiver.

After walking what Donny thought was an eternity, the sky colored pale yellow, light brown, and rose-red hues in the east. Maude said, "Let's stop and eat. I'm already homesick and we haven't gotten much past town." She handed Donny her parcel of bread and preserves and cooked potatoes. Then, looking at the sky in the east, she put her hands to her side and swayed in the breeze.

While Maude swayed, Terry reached to the side of her face with a cool hand. He wiped away a tear and, looking into the face of the woman he loved, quietly sang the first stanza of a famous Irish ballad.

"There's a tear in your eye,
And I'm wondering why,
For it never should be there at all.
With such pow'r in your smile
Sure a stone you'd beguile,

So there's never a teardrop should fall.
When your sweet lilting laughter's
Like some fairy song,
And your eyes twinkle bright as can be;
You should laugh all the while
And all other times smile,
And now, smile a smile for me."

"Terry, we won't ever come back, will we?"

Terry moved a curled lock to the side of Maude's face. "No. We probably won't."

"And we'll never see our loved ones again?" Maude had a pained look in her eyes.

"Honey, you have me and Donny. And you can keep in touch with everyone else through letters."

Maude started swaying again. Terry took her hand and led her to the side of the lane where Donny had opened the parcel of food and placed the contents on a level spot of a large boulder.

To improve Maude's spirits, Terry said, "Have you heard that Loren is thinking about getting married?"

"Really?"

"Yes and Dad's made a list of candidates he thinks Loren should consider. At the wake the other men started giving him their views. There should be some interesting times ahead for Loren."

"Do you think he would ever come to America?"

"No. Not as long as Mom and Dad are alive. Dad has officially turned over the farm to Loren, but Loren has to take care of them in return. He'll need a wife because Mother will soon be physically unable to do all the things she did in the past."

"I hope he makes that clear. Loren's a nice-looking man and now with a farm . . . still, the responsibility of taking care of the elderly is a daunting task, especially if she is also responsible for the upkeep of her own parents."

"It's still a man's world, isn't it?"

"Yes. I've noticed that a woman can get along quite well without a man, but a man founders without a woman."

148

Terry, Maude, and Donny finished their food and continued toward their new beginning. The sun rose and warmed their morning. Soon other travelers appeared. Most were pedestrians; some rode horses or bicycles.

At twenty minutes after seven the town opened its arms, showing them a water tower.

CHAPTER 38—ON THE TRAIN
Claremorris, Ireland, May 1909

In Claremorris the three wayfarers had no difficulty in purchasing their tickets and finding comfortable seats on the Westport Balling-Dublin Railway. Donny was wide-eyed as he climbed aboard for his first train ride. Terry stowed their suitcase while Maude surveyed her situation.

"Have they got accommodations for the passengers?"

Terry stopped. "Accommodations for what?"

Maude poked her husband in his ribs, "Terrence O'Reilly, you know what the accommodations are for. Do I have to spell it out for you?"

"Uh—no, I don't think so. The train stops at every little town, so you'll only have to wait at most thirty minutes. Sometimes not even that long. But you'll have to be ready as we're only there long enough to let off a few and to let on a few. Ten minutes tops unless we have to load freight."

"I can manage."

Terry turned to his son and said, "Soon we'll switch to the West Claire Railway. It's known for always being late. A great Irish composer by the name of Percy French wrote a song about it. It's called *Are Ye Right There Michael? Are Ye Right?* Let's see if I remember some of the words." Quietly Terry started singing to his son.

> *"You may talk of Columbus's sailing*
> *Across the Atlantical sea,*
> *But he never tried to go railing*
> *From Ennis as far as Kilkee.*
> *You run for the train in the morning,*
> *The excursion train starting at eight.*
> *You're there when the guard gives the warning,*
> *And there for an hour you'll wait.*

151

And while you're waiting in the train,
You'll hear the guard sing this refrain:

Are ye right there, Michael, are ye right?
Do you think that we'll be home before night?

Ye've been so long in startin',
That ye couldn't say for certain'
Still ye might now, Michael,
So ye might!"

"Why is the train always late, Daddy?"

"Lots of reasons: engine failure, re-fueling, an important passenger late in arriving, inefficiency in getting the passengers ticketed and boarded, or freight loaded."

A train official walked through taking tickets and stopped when he heard Terry singing. "That song, sir, has been the ruination of the West Claire Railway Line. They are the laughingstock."

"Yes. I know. They even sued Mr. French for libel. When the time came for the trial Mr. French didn't show. The judge waited the prescribed time and just before it was up, Mr. French dragged in. When questioned why he was so late Mr. French is reported to have said he had the misfortune of taking the West Claire Railway and, of course, it was late. The judge nodded his head and said, 'This court finds in favor of the defendant. Court dismissed.'"

Other passengers listened with muffled laughs as the ticket taker made his way. Terry continued, "Donny, did you notice the cars on the back end of the train? We're carrying cattle as well as people."

"Daddy, will the ship be carrying cattle too?"

"No. When the ships come to the British Isles and to Ireland from America, they carry bulky items. They bring mostly tobacco, cotton, and grain. But when they return to America they carry finished goods. The finished goods don't take up as much cargo space as the bulky items. And since the value of the goods brought have to be roughly the same in equivalent value as the items they are traded for, the ships have extra room on the trip to America. So the freight companies supplement their cargo with passengers—more going than coming.

"We'll buy steerage tickets, which means we get treated about the same as a sack of potatoes. Not much light, bad food, the accommodations your mother worries about will be almost non-existent, and we'll be squished together like sardines. And after a month of friendly relations with people you'll soon despise, we arrive at the most wonderful place in the world. Of course, those few weeks will be nerve-wracking. Still, it's not like a few years back when the ships were called 'coffin ships.' They were given that name because the conditions were so bad half the passengers didn't make it."

"But we're going to make it, aren't we?"

"Yes, son, I'll—we'll make it."

CHAPTER 39—THE TRAIN TRIP
Queenstown, Ireland, May 1909

Before Queenstown, Claremorris was the largest town Donny had ever seen. He couldn't understand how so many people could huddle together so closely. When he walked into his hometown of Cloonfad, it took an hour. If it rained, going into town took less than an hour with his dad and well over an hour with his mother or grandparents. They looked for shelter while his dad looked for collected water to splash through. Donny liked running through the rain with his dad the best.

Bicycles, cars, and trucks abounded in Queenstown. Other than Rob Matthews, nobody had an automobile in Cloonfad. The only other cars or trucks Donny had encountered were the ones he had to jump out of the way of as they came charging down the lane.

When the train pulled into the station Donny's mother stood at the front of the carriage. She was determined to be the first one off and the first one finding the accommodations she had missed on the previous four stops. Each time the need was a little more urgent and each time she was a little faster off the train and better at figuring the most likely location. She had even stopped asking directions. But when she arrived there was always somebody inside and a few others lined up in a queue waiting for their turn. Each time she had been faster than the time before. Each time there were fewer people waiting. Still when the whistle blew saying the train was about to pull out she had always still been in line.

But not this time. When the train came to a stop she didn't wait for the carriage attendant to open the carriage door. No, she opened it herself and descended in one hop instead of the customary three steps. Holding her skirt she was moving pretty fast until she saw another woman in a similar situation. Maude picked up speed and overtook her adversary twenty feet from the door. As she entered she called over her shoulder. "Sorry, I won't be but a minute."

When she exited the woman she had outrun ran inside. Six others waited. Her husband and son were off to one side. Terry was red in the face.

"You were pretty fast there, young lady. Donny and I saw several near collisions and this is the last stop. Everyone has plenty of time now."

"Then you don't understand the circumstances. It's not something you can casually schedule."

"Well, let's walk to the White Star Line's wharf and see when the next ship will leave." From a street vendor, Terry bought three skewers of meat on a stick and three cups of lemonade.

Donny was having a wonderful time. The streets were cobblestone with trucks, wheelbarrows, and horses pulling carts. businessmen carried small suitcases, fancy women wore hats, and kids played ball in the streets. Also, there were dogs and alley cats. Everything and everybody piled one on another.

Terry passed several places for lodging and made a mental note of the ones he thought clean enough to suit Maude. When they reached the wharf, a ship was tied from ropes extending from several places on the ship's deck to big brass plugs sticking up from wooden planks on the wharf. The ship had only one deck which was covered by an awning. Terry said, "I thought it would be bigger."

A man standing nearby said, "She is. This is the tender used to carry passengers out of the harbor, past Roche's Point with the lighthouse. It even goes beyond where the Daunt Rock on the west and the Cow and Calf Rocks on the east guard the entrance proper. That's where the ship's anchored and waiting on you and your family. She's entirely too big to come all the way in and tie up to our wharf. The Harbor Master won't let ships of her size past the lighthouse."

Terry thanked the Lord. He did not want his family to be quartered in one corner of the small ship in front of him. Not huddling together on a wet and windy deck as the little dingy fought the waves breaking across her bow as she plowed her way to America. To the man he said, "You work here?"

"No, I was going to be a passenger. But the tickets weren't meant for me they're yours. She sets sail tomorrow."

"I'm sorry. You said mine?"

"That's right. They quit selling tickets several days ago when the manifest filled. Me and my family were heading to America, but my wife changed her mind, saying she wasn't going. She left me holding three tickets. I can let you have them real cheap."

Terry looked at the man for a moment and said, "That's too bad . . . but we're heading to Prince Edward Island. So I guess we'll have to wait for a ship going to Canada."

"Oh, the SS *Adriatic's* going to Canada. It stays awhile in New York City then goes on up the coast. You'll just have to wait a couple of days to let them get most of their cargo off."

"I didn't think the English ships were welcome in the French harbors of Canada."

"Normally they're not, but this captain has been there a few times and slips the Harbor Master a fiver to let him in. Mind you, no one other than the passengers get off."

"I think I'll have to pass. Me and the family are on a holiday and we're not ready to go just yet."

"But you've got your suitcase."

"Just something to keep our purchases in. Good day, sir."

"And it's got a train tag on it."

Terry took Donny's hand and walked down the pier to see if he could see the lighthouse on Roche's Point. The ticket hawker left and walked to another couple standing nearby. When the O'Reillys walked back to the front of the pier, the second couple were looking closely at the tickets they had just purchased.

Terry said, "Are they real?"

The man put the tickets in his pocket and said, "I certainly hope so. I saw the bloke out here the day his wife stormed off saying she wasn't going. He had purchased three second class tickets: one for him, one for his wife, and one for his mother-in-law. If you ask me, I think he's better off. He sold them at little more than the price of steerage, taking a substantial loss, but saving himself years of anguish."

Terry turned to Maude. "I could have sworn he was a swindler and the tickets were counterfeit."

Maude said, "Honey, he might have been on the up and up, but without more information you had to go with your best judgment. We'll get tickets and we'll pay the right price."

At the ticket office window a posted notice said the SS *Adriatic* was full and it would be a week before a sister ship arrived. After milling around the wharf and looking in the store windows, Terry and his family backtracked to a convenient inn. He paid for three nights in their cheapest room.

CHAPTER 40—THE LAYOVER
Queenstown, Ireland, June 1909

The lodging Terry had chosen was Jury's Cork Inn. Their room came with a complimentary breakfast of meats and fruits and stemmed glasses of pudding. Terry and Maude drank cups of steaming coffee and Donny swigged a glass of milk. Terry thought this was the life, but he'd have to be careful that Donny and Maude didn't come to expect this extravagant living on a regular basis.

On a table in the reception area were maps of the city and brochures giving walking directions to the city's attractions. Terry took a map and a brochure and led his family outside, where each could look at the brochure and request places to visit.

Donny said, "Dad, here's a fire station. Can we see what they have? And here . . ." Donny pointed to another entry on the brochure, "they have a toy museum."

Maude said, "I'd like to walk up and down the shopping area. The stores might be fun to browse through, but the real interest for me is watching the people."

"Honey, we'll do all these things, but first we have to make it to the ticket office for White Star Lines so I can buy our tickets for their next ship to America."

On the way to the ticket office, the O'Reillys passed through the English Market where vendors sold fruits and vegetables. Terry bought a sack of grapes and gave them to Donny. At the ticket office they were told no one could purchase tickets without passports from the country they were leaving and visas for the country they were traveling to. They received a letter with instructions for obtaining the needed documents.

Looking at the sheet, Terry said, "Honey, do you have our birth certificates with you?"

Maude said, "Yes, and Donny's school transcripts and all our medical records."

"You are a wonderment." Shaking the sheet he said, "We should take care of this as soon as possible."

They arrived at the main post office and on the second floor were the offices for the Irish Department of Immigration. It was a bustling office filled mostly with young ladies and the occasional supervisor. Terry got in a queue, filled out a form, and was told to take a seat. He would be called for an interview.

In a few minutes a woman walked to the tray holding the forms and shuffled through before picking one out. She had caught Terry's attention by the way everyone deferred to her as she passed—they were getting out of her way. Over the counter she looked straight at Terry and said, "Terrence O'Reilly."

Terry had walked around the room looking at the pictures on the walls and reading the brass plaques attached to each. He had not expected his name to be called so fast. Other people still waiting had been there when he and his family arrived.

Terry walked up clutching the documents Maude gave him. "I'm Terry O'Reilly."

"Follow me, Mr. O'Reilly. Have you and your family had your pictures taken?"

"Not yet." Terry entered a bland office containing a desk, three chairs, and two filing cabinets. He sat in an upright wooden chair in front of her desk. The woman's desk was clean, with only his form on its surface.

"Mr. O'Reilly, may I see the birth certificates and medical records please? Now, Mr. O'Reilly, when will you be needing your passports?"

"As soon as possible. We want to travel to America on the next ship."

"I see. Well, Mr. O'Reilly, it normally takes two to three weeks to get your passport processed. Have you procured lodging?"

"I have, but it will take my entire savings if I have to stay there three weeks. Is there not something I can do to speed things up?"

"There might be. If you did something to . . . to impress me. I might work extra hard—even through my lunch. If I did that, I could probably have them for you by tomorrow afternoon."

"What do you mean, impress you?"

"Mr. O'Reilly, this is a boring job. If you could make my day a little more memorable, I would return the favor."

"Do you have any suggestions?"

"No."

Terry thought a minute, then set his hat on the desk and stepped away from the chair. From his pocket he took a purple velvet bag with yellow corded drawstrings. From the bag he slid out a harmonica and played the first few notes of a national ballad. After the harmonica introduction he sang in a soft, expressive, tenor voice,

"Oh Danny boy, the pipes, the pipes are calling
From glen to glen, and down the mountain side
The summer's gone, and all the roses falling
'Tis you, 'tis you must go, and I must bide."

Terry played a few more lines with the harmonica and continued singing with,

"But come you back when summer's in the
meadow
Or when the valley's hushed and white with
snow
'Tis I'll be there in sunshine or in shadow
Oh Danny boy, oh Danny boy, I love you so."

A new employee took hold of a supervisor's arm and whispered, "My God, that's beautiful. What's going on?"

His reply was, "Myrna is just breaking the monotony. Yesterday she had a guy dance in his socks on her desk. And last week a man started taking off his clothes. We had to stop him."

All the women put down what they were doing and listened. They removed handkerchiefs from purses and patted their eyes dry or blew their noses. In the reception area mothers shushed their children.

Donny asked, "Is Daddy singing to the lady?"

"I believe ge is," said Maude. "We'll probably be walking out of here with those passports."

A moment after the singing had stopped Terry made it back to the reception area and said, "Come on, we have to have our pictures taken."

Maude winked at Donny. "See. I told you."

On the sidewalk, they continued to take on energy from a thriving city with a contagious spirit of free enterprise.

While waiting for Maude to visit a public accommodation, Terry read about the Cork City *Gaol*. According to the brochure the *gaol* was once over-populated with prisoners quartered in miserable conditions. Hunger will drive a man to do things he would not normally consider and the gaol was full of such men. One punishment given to recalcitrant inmates was to walk a treadmill.

The brochure said that the overflow of criminals was now housed in converted old ships anchored in the harbor. Such were the penalties for stealing to feed your family. Terry shuddered.

Butter was Ireland's most important food export. With Queenstown built on a naturally deep-water harbor, she became the place for the Butter Exchange: where butter was graded, bought and sold, and warehoused before being shipped around the world. Over half a million casks of butter went out from Queenstown each year. But Donny and Maude were not interested in visiting the Butter Exchange. During the course of the next hour, they went to the Crawford Municipal Art Gallery and stepped inside to eat at a restaurant run by the Ballymaloe Cookery School.

Next to the art gallery was the Coal Quay on the banks of the north fork of the Lee River. Turning right they headed to the Merchant's Quay and spent the rest of the day taking in the sights of a bustling retail area.

That night Terry counted his money. They were not being frivolous, but the food and lodging would soon be making major inroads into his purse. He had separated the portion of his funds he planned on spending for travel tickets and had already been into that compartment for their train ride. He was now thinking he might should have worked another year. Surely the train would be building another spur somewhere. Well, so be it. They were committed. They would have to economize.

Their third day in Queenstown they headed back to the post office where Maude said, "You guys can loiter here while I go inside to check on the passports."

She returned in fifteen minutes or less and said they would be ready right after lunch. She suggested they go to the United States Consular Office to get the visas. This time she would talk with the clerk.

"Maude, did I embarrass you?"

"No." Tears came to Maude's eyes. "Terry, why do you let people run all over you?"

"No one ran all over me. The normal wait for passports is three weeks. We couldn't wait that long. She said if I could do something interesting she would work through lunch and get me the passports before closing the next day. Maude, in three weeks we wouldn't have enough money left to purchase tickets. This place is sucking my purse dry. To sing her a song was not so much to offer."

"Dad, did you know women cry when you sing? I think you sound wonderful, but it must make them sad."

By late afternoon Maude had both the passports and their visas in her pocket and it was time to find a restaurant for their evening meal.

The morning after the third night, they returned to the White Star Ticketing Office with their passports, visas, and single suitcase. After purchasing their tickets, they needed to find cheaper lodging.

"Mr. O'Reilly, I'm required to ask you a few questions. Bring your family and step into my office." After everyone was comfortably seated the ticket agent opened a form and started penning their names onto the proper blank spaces. "I got twenty-eight more questions, then we'll handle the ticket purchase. Do you need a place to stay while you wait on the SS *Celtic*?"

"How much will it cost?"

"The ticket prices were listed on the sheet I gave you two days ago, but lodging for passengers with tickets is free."

"That is terrific. Utterly fantastic. What's the next question?"

For thirty minutes the agent pried into the lives of the O'Reillys. He wanted to know the name of their nearest relative in Ireland, what kind of work they were qualified for, the literacy of all three, if either one had ever had a major or contagious illness, if mental illness ran in either of their extended families, if Terry had ever been incarcerated or put into an almshouse, and how much money they had. Twenty-nine questions and the O'Reilly's felt weary and violated when the questioning was done.

The agent said, "Let me get the boy a glass of water. Is there anything you'd like to know about the trip or the ship?"

"Yeah, how long will she be in port before leaving? What do we need to bring? How long will the trip take? What kind of sleeping arrangements are provided? What . . ."

"Whoa. Let me start at the beginning. The ship will be in port for two days after it arrives and food comes with the ticket, but you might want to bring additional items to add variety to the ship's fare. The third class passengers, that's what steerage passengers are now called, will start ferrying to the ship from our spot on the wharf at ten in the morning on the day of departure. Normally the ship will sail in the middle of that same afternoon.

"The trip to the United States originated in Liverpool. Queenstown is the ship's first stop and she will be taking on additional freight here. The deck for third class is directly above the cargo area so you can't board until the additional freight has been stowed."

Donny sat on the edge of his seat. He knew this was important and if something was missed, his father could ask him.

"She'll arrive in Queenstown about sixty percent full. When you go aboard find an empty berth the right size for your family or a larger berth with the correct number of vacant bunks. We got some with two beds but most are four and six-bed berths. We also got a few with eight bunks, but we hold them for large families. We're gonna be sailing full, so someone will occupy every bed. Families are in the middle section. Single men are forward in a separate section. The single women sleep aft. Each section has its own entrance, washrooms, and toilets. Linens, towels, blankets, and pillows are all furnished. And the dining is a sit-down affair served by stewards."

Terry was dumbfounded. This was not what he had expected. He had heard stories of people packed in like matchsticks in a box. He had certainly not expected his family to be given a separate berthing compartment.

The agent looked at a confused family. "I know. It's a lot different sailing on one of these new steamships. Just a few years back we packed everybody in and, I'm sorry to say, conditions were not the most sanitary. The food, if any was provided, was of poor quality. But things have changed. Legislation and the opportunity to make a decent profit made the steamship companies revamp their ship designs. You know, third class now has lighting in each compartment and separate storage for your baggage. Twenty years ago, no kerosene lamps were allowed below decks and you had to bring your own bedding. You also had to prepare your own food. It was a month of hell. Now we make the trip in luxury and it only takes eight to ten days."

When the meeting ended Maude placed their three tickets in her pocket with the passports and visas. A taxi took them to White Star's lodging which was dormitory style. But being free has its advantages. The O'Reillys had averted a financial disaster. Now they could enjoy their last few days in Ireland without fear of decimating their stash and arriving in America without funds. The room they were in held about fifty people, but only ten others were there. A take-charge Maude commandeered an entire corner.

After eating a free meal Terry, Maude, and Donny made a trip to the English Market. Maude said she wanted to plan her purchases, since only foods that would carry well and not go bad without refrigeration could be purchased. At the market Maude made a list of what would work. Continuing up the street they shopped in several shops on the Market Quay, but each time a shopkeeper asked if he could help he was told they were only looking. One was a bookseller and Donny made a mental note that if they came back he would ask for something to read on the trip.

After being notified of the arrival of the SS *Celtic* and of the day she would depart, Terry and Maude planned, schemed, budgeted, and ruminated over the remainder of their trip. Back at the bookseller they looked for books about life in America. Terry bought two books for Donny. One was Treasure Island by Robert Louis Stephenson and the other was Ivanhoe by Sir Walter Scott. It was a magical time and years later they would look back with fond remembrances of their last few days in the Emerald Isles.

CHAPTER 41—BLARNEY CASTLE
Queenstown, Ireland, June 1909

Lying in bed, Terry stroked his fingers through Maude's hair. She opened her eyes and placed her hand on his. Softly Terry said, "Maude, I'd like to take you and Donny to see a famous rock. You may never get another chance and everyone Irish needs to see it sometime in their lifetime."

"Are you talking about the Blarney Stone?"

"I am. When I was three, misery stalked the land. We struggled: hardly anything to eat, most of the potato crop slimy with blight, Mother pregnant with Loren, and Dad expecting Lord Chaney to give our small tenancy to someone else. So much anguish, so many people with down-trodden expressions, so much despair, I was traumatized. I didn't talk— had never talked. I walked around like a zombie.

Dad decided I had to kiss the Blarney Stone. He thought that was their only hope to ever hear me say something. It took us ten days to complete the journey. When we got to Blarney Castle, Dad took my hand and led me up a long, winding staircase. I felt like Isaac must have felt when Abraham prepared him for sacrifice. No one had told me anything about what was so important about this rock. I didn't say anything, so there was no reason for anyone to carry on a one-sided conversation with me."

"Did it work?"

"Well honey, what do you think?"

"Oh, I know you can talk—and you have the most wonderful pitch and tonality to your speech. But is it because you kissed the Blarney Stone?"

"I don't know. But I would sure like to visit it one more time. To say—to say goodbye."

"How far is it? Will we have to take the train?"

"No. It's five miles north and a little west of Queenstown. If we pack a lunch it'll be a one-day adventure. We could eat a big breakfast before leaving and be back in time for the evening meal."

The next morning Maude talked to one of the staff. When the O'Reillys finished breakfast Maude was handed a small box with a handle. She was told it was enough to see the three of them through till the evening meal.

It was a wonderful day and the sun shone brightly. Terry had a hand-drawn map, Maude the boxed lunch, and Donny carried rocks in his pockets in case he got an opportunity to get in some target practice.

Three blocks away from their new lodging, Maude asked Terry to carry the boxed lunch and after another two blocks Donny asked his parents to wait while he divested himself of the heavy ballast chafing his leg. By the time they reached the outskirts of Queenstown, Maude suggested they find a vendor selling refreshments. What had started out as a beautiful day with the sun shining brightly quickly turned into a sweltering summer day. The sun beat down thick with rays of suffocating heat.

At ten in the morning, Terry purchased a lemonade for Donny and two pints of Guinness for him and Maude. At one in the afternoon they purchased more beverages. Under a sprawling oak tree in Blarney Village they took a break, ate the boxed lunch, and drank two more beverages each. By the time they walked the few blocks to Blarney castle Maude felt light-headed. She found a bench outside the keep to rest on and suggested that Terry and Donny climb the stairs to the top of the battlements. She told her husband he would have his hands full holding Donny by his ankles while he dangled sixty-five feet up trying to kiss a dirty old stone and he could not devote any time to keep her from losing her balance and rolling off the other side.

"Maude, there's a little rock garden close by. It's shady, has a stream meandering through, and there are lots of large rocks for sitting. When Dad brought me, we stayed there for a couple of hours waiting for the attendant to arrive to do his day of work at the rock. They don't let you kiss the rock unless you're on a guided tour. Dad thought we had an hour or so to kill and we took a short nap. It's a magical place called the Rock Close."

"Wow. A nap sounds wonderful."

About that time a cloud came up and blocked the sun. Thirty minutes later Terry deposited a slightly inebriated Maude in the Rock

Close as the sky grew dark and threatened a summer shower. "I'll come get you in a few minutes. Be careful a rock in here is supposed to be the prison for a witch. And that rock over there is a sacrificial stone used by the Druids hundreds of years ago." Terry pointed to a rock slab, but Maude's eyes were already closed.

Soon the air got thin and cool. Mist descended to make things uncomfortable for Maude. She stirred as an elderly man wadded up his hat and stuffed it under her head. He unbuttoned his cape and carefully placed it over Maude's body as she had drawn up her feet and was now completely curled on top of the big rock.

Sleepily, Maude murmured, "Thank you."

"Think nothing of it. It's not often I'm visited by someone quite as lovely as you. Do you mind telling me how old you are? I would like to know at what age a woman is most beautiful."

Maude sat up. "Am I dreaming?"

"Possibly."

"I'm old enough to know better than to be alone with the King of the Leprechauns."

"Lassie, I'm no king of anything. I'm Cormac McCarthy. Welcome to my home."

"You live here?" Maude looked around for a house.

"Well, not exactly here, but you are on my property."

"You own the Blarney Stone?"

"It was given to me by Robert the Bruce after I supplied four thousand men to fight beside him at the battle of Bannockburn. Most people don't know this, but it was originally part of the Stone of Scone."

"And . . ."

"And, lassie, the Stone of Scone is used in the coronation of the monarchs of Scotland. It's also known as the Stone of Destiny."

"I've heard it was Jacob's pillow and brought to Ireland by the prophet Jeremiah."

"The church is always trying to incorporate anything revered by the people into their lore."

"So the rumor that it was brought over during the Crusades and taken from the Wailing Wall is also false."

"Yes, as well as the story of it being the Stone of Ezel. David hid behind that stone on Jonathan's advice, while he fled from the wrath of King Saul. Also, it is not the stone that gushed water after being struck by Moses."

"What about its mystical powers?"

"What do you think of your husband's singing?"

"It's wonderful. The women swoon. They have been known to faint. Just listening to him talk is enough to make me curl my toes with excitement."

"Was he able to do that before he kissed the stone?"

"No. He said he never talked before he kissed the Blarney Stone."

"I rest my case."

"Mr. McCarthy, how did you know about that?"

"Lassie, tell me about you. What can I do for you?"

"I just want my two boys safe."

"Spoken like a woman in love. In a minute you'll go back to sleep. When you wake, walk up and back down the Witch's Steps backwards with your eyes closed. All the while you must think of your wish. When you leave, go to the Witch's Stone and thank her for she is the one who will make your wish come true. It's good for one year."

Maude laid her head back on the rock and drew up her feet. Soon she was deep in sleep and still slumbering when Terry found her. "Honey, wake up. You haven't seen the Blarney Stone yet."

Maude yawned, raised herself on an elbow, yawned again, and sat facing her husband and son. She put her hands to both sides of her head shaking the cobwebs and slowly said, "I have to find the Witch's Steps."

Thirty minutes later, with her eyes closed, she had managed to walk backwards a series of stone rectangular blocks arranged in a stair-step fashion. Going up and coming back down she focused her mind on the request of safety for Terry and Donny.

"What did he look like? Was he a slight man with long hair? Did he wear brown baggy pants stuffed in old-fashioned boots that reached up past his knees?"

"Yes. Yes, that's exactly what he looked like. Have you seen him?"

"He was here the first time I kissed the Blarney Stone."

170

"That is so weird. Show me the Witch's Stone."

After Maude had thanked the witch imprisoned in a stone and run her hands over it like she was smoothing the wrinkles from her bedding, she and her family went to the keep and joined another group ascending the staircase to kiss the rock. When it became Maude's turn, she sat on the precipice with her back facing the chasm. Terry secured her ankles with a tight grip while she scooted backwards. Soon the only part of her still on the battlement was her legs. As she dangled over the side, Maude asked the attendant, "Is this the Blarney Stone?" She pointed to a rock larger than others in the wall and jutting out like it was secured in a place of prominence.

"Yes. That's it."

CHAPTER 42—THE SS *CELTIC*
Laying off Roches Point, Ireland, June 1909

Terry, Maude, and Donny were on the wharf an hour early. A rope stretched in front of three gangplanks with tags saying "No Admittance."

Terry mumbled, "We may have to wait a spell."

"Daddy, how big is the ship?"

"She's big, son. I read in the brochure that she was the largest ship in the world for a couple of years. She can handle two thousand passengers sailing third class."

"Will we get sea-sick?"

"Maybe not. As long as she is, we'll probably straddle several wave crests at a time. I think getting sea-sick is from going up one and down another. Also we are in the middle compartment which should limit the heaving. The single men forward and the single women aft will go up higher and down lower on each heave."

"And you thought that up all by yourself?" asked Maude.

"Yep. I'm more than a man with a golden throat."

"I agree, and you're all mine. Still, I think your information is suspect."

At ten o'clock stewards in white uniforms went to the ends of the gangplanks and removed the three signs. With each trip a hundred passengers were ferried from the small inland harbor with the pier through the much larger Cork Harbor proper. Standing in the tender's prow on the first trip, Terry, Maude, and Donny could see from Cork Harbor the lighthouse guarding the harbor entrance. They passed through the narrow inlet into the Atlantic Ocean. Under a clear sky waited the magnificent ship they would be sailing to that great land of opportunity.

"Donny, look. There she is."

"Daddy, I don't understand how something that big can float on water."

"You'll learn that in school some day. And when you do, be sure to tell me."

The tender pulled alongside the SS *Celtic* and tied off stern and aft. A gangplank extended from an opening in the side and was fastened to a receptacle on the tender. The passengers walked up the gangplank into the side of the ship, where they were led upwards to the lowest open deck. The man herding them along said this was their strolling deck. He then guided them to the three third class berthing entrances.

"Donny, stay with your mother while I find an empty four-bed berth." Terry returned and led his family down a corridor before opening a door into a small enclosed space with two bunk beds on the left and two on the right. A small table was attached to the back wall in the center. A switch on the wall operated a weak light in the center of the ceiling. There were no windows or, in the maritime jargon, portholes.

Above the table, Terry found a cupboard door with a mirror attached. He opened it and peered inside. "Must be for the stowage of luggage." He plopped down on one of the lower beds and said, "This is fantastic. I had anticipated being thrown in a hole with only enough floor space to huddle together while we tried to stay dry and warm while warding off sickness and disease. The man who sold us our tickets said how things had changed, but I still couldn't quite believe it. Well, I believe it now."

Maude stuffed her sack of fruit into the storage compartment. "And it's only going to take eight to ten days to get there." She closed the compartment asking, "Do you know the procedure for being admitted into America?"

"Just the barest of information. We'll have to ask."

At noon the last deposit of passengers arrived and they scrambled to find the empty beds left. What they found was a lot of single beds. Families of two, three, and four had taken the four-bed berths leaving, at most, one or two empty beds, families of five and six commandeered the six-bed berths leaving at most one empty bed, and families of seven and eight took the eight-bed berths that were left. The families late arriving had to split up.

A woman opened their door and looked around before asking, "May my daughter have your fourth bed?"

Maude said, "Sure. Does she need any help with her baggage?" But the lady had already left, looking for a second bed.

"Come in honey. What's your name?"

A girl in her early teens said, "Meghan. Which is mine?"

Terry said, "Which one do you want?"

"This one." Meghan threw the sack she was carrying onto the right top bunk.

"Meghan . . ." Maude held out her hand, "we are the O'Reillys. My name is Maude, this is Donny . . ." she pointed to her son. "And this is my husband . . ." she put her hand on Terry's shoulder, "Terry O'Reilly."

"Pleased to meet you. Do you know when we'll eat?"

Donny thought Meghan was about two years older than he and half a foot taller. He had never been around many girls. His classmates were mostly boys. Lots of girls didn't go to school. He wondered how the privacy issue would play out. There wasn't a washroom inside the berth. It must be in the common area. But still, there would be undressing and dressing and sleeping and snoring. Do girls snore? Donny knew his mother did sometimes—when she had the sniffles.

Later Meghan's mother came back and knocked before entering. Terry and Donny had gone exploring while Maude and Meghan lay down. After they exchanged pleasantries, Meghan's mother, named Norah, explained that they were headed to New York City to meet her husband. He had emigrated there eighteen months earlier and sent for them to join him. Norah was a handsome woman, tall and willowy, and entirely too lenient with Meghan. Maude had already made up her mind that Meghan was a rebellious youth with an attitude. She hardly spoke to her mother feigning sleep in a top bunk.

"Norah, do you know anything about the procedures upon arrival?"

"Yes, first there is the quarantine, then the ferry to Ellis Island where you fill out the forms, get a physical examination, get asked a lot of silly questions, and then board a train to New York City. The only thing you have to look out for is letting someone mark on your blouse with colored chalk. They'll send you back if that happens."

175

Maude said, "Why would they want to do that?"

"I don't know, but if I see a guy walking around with a stick of chalk I'm going the other direction."

For the noon meal Meghan went her own way. Maude thought Meghan might be looking for her mother, until Norah sat down with a tray of food professing not to know where Meghan was. The meal was filling but decidedly tasteless. Terry suggested that the passengers were of different nationalities and catering to each would be inefficient. So each group should season to their own taste. When the agent selling them their tickets suggested Maude bring additional food, he might have meant seasoning.

Maude pointed to a cordoned off area, "Like those?"

"I think those might be Jews. Their food has to be kosher and prepared ritualistically. If you'll notice, besides being separated by that ribbon, they also have their own servers. Probably their own cook too."

"Norah, if there is anything we can do to help you with Meghan?" Maude looked straight in Norah's face.

"Thank you. I've had a hard time raising the girl. She has a stubborn streak second only to her father's. Just keep an eye on her. If she does anything to bother you, let me know. I'll talk to her."

About five in the afternoon the crew raised the anchor, someone sounded the horn, and the SS *Celtic* started slowly moving on calm waters in a westerly direction. Terry, Maude, and Donny went as far forward as their open deck would allow and leaned against the railing to watch the waves slap against the bulkhead. A few minutes later, they went aft to see the wake they were leaving. It was a pleasant experience.

The rest of the afternoon Meghan was not around. When she did show she crawled into her bunk and slept through the evening meal.

CHAPTER 43—ON BOARD
Atlantic Ocean, June 1909

The second day of the trip, the third class passengers were told they would be checked by the ship's doctor on the following day. Norah told Maude she wouldn't participate as she had come down with a bad case of nausea and couldn't get far from her bed or the water closet. Norah's eyes were swollen and she walked with a side-ways limp.

Meghan left after the morning meal. Terry and Maude found chairs on the strolling deck and began reading their novels. Donny played with the other children but soon found he would rather practice with his yo-yo. His uncle Loren had shown him how to do a few tricks and he was deep into perfecting his craft. He could walk the dog, swing the baby in the cradle, and go around the world. The other children were amazed at his talent. Donny set aside his ambition to be a priest in favor of being a vaudeville entertainer.

That evening Meghan showed up just in time to sack out. Maude and Terry took special note but didn't say anything. Maude decided she should say something to Norah and let the two of them hash it out.

The third day, after the morning meal, the third class strolling deck was cleared of all passengers except the single men. Three stewards combed their berthing area to make sure all were there to be checked by the ship's doctor. After the single men were checked and told to go to their berthing area or to a special smoking room it was time to perform the same procedure on the single women.

Right before the noon meal, Maude checked on Norah. She was sweating profusely. "Maude, I can't get out of bed. Maybe the doctor could give me a clean bill of health here."

"You've got to be kidding. I'm going after him right now. I think you might have something worse than sea-sickness."

Norah grabbed Maude's arm, "Please don't. They'll ship me back. There's a whole list of sicknesses people can have that will keep them from being accepted by the authorities in America. I don't want to go back. There's nothing for me there."

"Okay. Have you had this before?"

"Yes. Tell Meghan to come see me. She'll know what to do."

When Maude returned, Meghan was no where to be found. She had left before the morning meal and had not been seen by anyone. Maude told Terry, "You've got to find where Meghan is going. Next time she leaves follow her. Do a little sleuthing like your friend Sherlock Holmes."

After the noon meal, and Meghan still had not been found, the families gathered on the promenade deck. Two orderlies held the unchecked passengers separate from the checked ones by a bright orange rope. To go from one side of the rope to the other the passengers were asked questions about their health and had their eyes checked by a nurse. Then they filed past a seated doctor, ascended a series of steps, walked across a bulkhead, and descended a series of steps on the other side. Most passengers received check-marks beside their names. Occasionally a passenger had something written instead. An orderly from below brought a list of passengers too sick to attend the physical examination. Maude assumed Norah was on the list.

After the examination and everyone was excused, Maude made her way to Norah's berth. When she got there, an orderly stood outside the door saying no one would be admitted until the doctor had finished. The door opened and a nurse shot out. She returned in a few minutes with two orderlies bringing a stretcher. All activity stopped and quiet coated the air as Norah was carried topside on the stretcher. Maude couldn't get close enough to say anything but vowed to do what she could to help Meghan.

When she got back to her own berth, no one was there. She went inside and ate an apple. Then she opened her book. It was at a particularly good spot in the story, but Maude couldn't focus. She worried about Norah, about Meghan, and now the remaining members of her family were missing, so she worried about them.

Two hours later Terry and Donny slumped in. Terry said, "Right after you left, we caught sight of Meghan and followed as best we could. She walked around the deck from front to back and down both sides three times. There were a lot of people and she finally got away from us. You know, with all the machinery, there are numerous hiding places. How about you? Did you get to talk with Norah?"

"No, they took her to the medical quarters. I think they have a sick room up there where they can watch more closely those really needing it."

"That's good. They'll know more about what ails her than somebody without the proper training."

"I know, but somehow I feel I've let her down. And I can't even keep up with her child."

"Donny and I will help you with that. We just had a trial run. We'll do better next time. Now why don't you go up and see if the doctor will talk to you about her."

"All right, but you be here when I get back. Here, have an apple."

That night Meghan came to bed reeking of spirits. She climbed into her bunk above Maude's with her clothes still on. Maude said, "Meghan, your mother is real sick. Do you know what might be wrong with her?"

"She shivering and sweating at the same time?"

"Might be. She also has puffy eyes and is sick to her stomach."

"She has spells like that sometimes. It comes and goes. In a couple of days she'll be back to normal."

"Honey, they took her to the medical area so they could keep an eye on her. The doctor thinks it's a combination of sea-sickness and something else. He has her quarantined and won't let anyone in. I told his assistant I would bring you by tomorrow to answer a few questions."

"I don't know nothing. I don't want to go."

"He's not going to make you stay with her. He just wants to know the symptoms so he can figure out what she's got and give her the correct medicine."

"I'll think about it."

CHAPTER 44—GHASTLY ENCOUNTER
Atlantic Ocean, June 1909

The next morning Meghan was still asleep when the O'Reillys finished getting dressed. Maude said, "You two go ahead. See if you can bring me and Meghan something back. In the meantime I'll stay so she won't slip out and stay gone all day."

In a few minutes Meghan stirred. She sat up and rubbed the sleep from her eyes. "The boys will soon be back bringing us biscuits and a sausage or two. Do you need to borrow a bar of soap?"

"Soap? No, I don't need no soap."

"We've got to go see the doctor. You need to be clean with a change of clothing. What you're wearing reeks of alcohol."

Meghan descended from her bunk and got in Maude's face. She said, "Lay off, bitch. No one tells me what to do."

Maude reached up and smacked Meghan with the back of her hand. Meghan's head snapped sideways. When she looked back she had the face of a frightened little girl with a red blotch on her cheek. Meghan started crying. When Maude tried to console her Meghan pulled away.

"Grab a towel. You're going to bathe."

Between sobs Meghan said, "You leave me alone. You can't make me."

Maude yanked Meghan up by her arm. Then, holding her with one hand, she opened the door to the compartment and dragged Meghan out. Meghan went reluctantly, soon realizing that Maude was a stronger woman and of a singular mind. Meghan was going to take a bath, no ifs, ands, or buts about it.

In the women's washroom were four shower stalls. Half of the two thousand third class passengers were females and half of those were in the larger of the three third class berthing areas. Four stalls for five hundred women. Maude thought she would say something to the authorities. Maybe if there were enough complaints the next class of ships would have adequate facilities.

"Get your hair wet then rub this in all the way down to the scalp. Do it right and we'll be finished in no time. Do it slipshod and I'll do it for you."

"Okay. Okay. Let me get the water warmer."

"Now rinse that out and lather your entire body with this. When was the last time you had a bath?"

"A few days ago."

"Use a wash cloth. Scrub until your hide turns pink."

"You a school teacher or something?"

"No. A mother who doesn't put up with insolent children. You ready to come out of there?"

"No. Not just yet."

By the time Meghan towel-dried her hair and dressed, the boys returned with two plates of food. As Meghan downed the last biscuit covered with milk gravy, Maude said, "If you will allow it, I'd like to go with you to see the medical officer."

"If you have to."

"Donny, you and your dad tidy things up while Meghan and I go find out what's wrong with Norah. I shouldn't be very long." She looked at Terry reading a book. "Donny, you're in charge."

Donny picked up the two dirty plates and headed out the door. Terry looked over the top of his book and surveyed the state of the compartment. He continued reading as Meghan and Maude left. He had decided that cleaning the compartment would be a quick chore and could easily be put off.

At the medical officer's office, Maude and Meghan were given chairs and the officer pulled a tablet of blank paper from a desk drawer. Norah's file lay on the desk unopened. The officer looked at Meghan and said, "You are the daughter?"

"Yes. My name is Meghan."

"Good. And you are?" He looked at Maude.

"Maude O'Reilly, a friend."

"I see. Do either of you know if the patient has ever had a similar episode?"

Meghan said, "Yes, sir. My dad sent us ticket money about six months ago, but Mother used part of the money to buy something for me. It was her plan to sell most of our stuff, with us only taking a few clothes on the trip. She thought she would replace the spent money when she had made a few sales. But no one wanted to buy any of our things and she had to get a job working in one of the taverns on the wharf. She started having spells soon after starting work."

"I see. Meghan, your mother is terribly sick. Her condition has deteriorated since we first got her here. I now have her resting as comfortably as possible, but she has a high fever, diarrhea, and sometimes she loses consciousness while her body fights the malady. I don't know what she's sick with but suspect it's cholera or one of the tropical diseases she might have been exposed to from an infected sailor. It might even be yellow fever."

"May I see her?"

"Have you had any episodes yourself?"

"No. Not one."

"Then, yes. You may see her. Evidently you are immune. You have been exposed over a long period of time and have not exhibited any symptoms. But Mrs. O'Reilly will have to talk to her through a glass partition.

When Maude and Meghan returned, Donny was waiting. He and his mother headed to the open deck with their books. Terry left to occupy an advantageous spot supporting a good view of both the compartment door and the stairs leaving the berthing area. He was in for a boring afternoon as Meghan climbed into her bunk and cried herself to sleep.

Maude sported a wide-brimmed sun hat to shade her fair complexion. She had a book to read but couldn't seem to get interested in the story. Most of the day she watched other passengers walk past her lounging chair. Donny finished Treasure Island and was now working on Ivanhoe in an adjacent chair.

That night, after midnight, Meghan quietly descended from her top bunk and stole out the compartment door. Donny had been waiting and followed a few seconds later. When he opened the door its hinges squeaked, but no one stirred. Donny thought being a private detective might be his occupation of choice. He quickly replaced the vaudeville circuit entertaining crowds by means of a mesmerizing yo-yo performance with an adrenalin-pumping vocation as a high-profile gumshoe.

In the dark of the corridor, he made his way toward the stairs leading to the open deck. He could barely make out movement in the distance. Meghan negotiated through the darkness faster than he and had lengthened her lead. When Donny opened the door at the top of the stairs, he stepped into a fog that reduced his sight to the length of his arm. The deck was well-lit, illuminating the darkness into a light haze just as impenetrable. In the distance he heard people talking. With his hands stuck out in front to keep him from bumping into the machinery or bulkheads Donny slowly made his way toward the noise.

"Hal, please don't."

"What do you mean, please don't? Do you know what happens to little princesses who tease and never please?"

"I didn't promise you anything. Hal, don't put your hand there. Hal. Please, Hal."

"You know you want it. Quit squirming so much. Ow." Donny heard a slap, then crying. "That'll teach you to bite me."

Meghan sobbed as she said, "Please stop. I never meant for you—don't Hal. I have to go back. I only came out to tell you I wasn't coming anymore." There was more noise. It sounded like two people were wrestling on a mat.

Donny increased his speed. Stumbling on a man's outstretched foot, Donny stopped then leaned forward and saw Meghan was down on the deck with a man on top. He had her hands pinned. Donny jumped on his back and, grabbing his head from behind, gouged at the man's eyes.

"Ow. Get the hell off me." The man reached around, seized Donny by the arm, and slung him across the deck. Donny picked up a folded deck chair and came back, slamming it into the back of the man still on top of Meghan.

"Damnit it, kid. You and—" Donny hit the man in the head with the chair. The man rolled off and looked through the fog for his adversary. "Kid, when I get a hold of you, you're history." The man felt the side of his face for blood as he searched for his attacker. Donny hid under an air vent protruding through the deck. When the man got close enough and facing away Donny stepped from his hiding spot and whopped the deck chair against the man's ankle. The man yelled in pain and grabbed a badly bruised foot that was beginning to swell at the ankle. He fell to the deck. Donny swung again, but this time the man grabbed the chair and yanked it away. Donny let go and rolled away.

The man stumbled to his feet and lunged at Donny. "I'll feed you to the fishes." Donny was up, he feinted left, then darted to the man's right, running into the railing on the perimeter of the deck. Donny fell back.

Hearing the collision, the man charged forward yelling, "I've got you now, buster" The man lunged to grab Donny before he made another escape. Donny bolted sideways and the man ran into the railing. Donny had hit the railing with his chest, getting knocked backwards. But the man hit it with his stomach and tumbled over. Meghan and Donny heard the man scream as he fell forty feet into a watery abyss.

Meghan put her hand on Donny's shoulder. "What do we do now?"

"We can tell someone or we can keep it to ourselves. Either way, the man's dead."

"I'd rather we told someone."

"Okay. You go back to the compartment and I'll ring the emergency bell."

Soon a steward ushered Donny into the security officer's quarters. "Sit down and tell me what happened."

"Well, sir, I went up on deck to look for a book I had left and saw a man standing on the railing. I walked toward him and he yelled for me to get back. Then he lost his balance and fell over the side."

"Was he wearing a life preserver?"

"No."

"And he didn't say anything other than for you to get back?"

"No, sir. That's all. Are you going back to rescue him?"

"No. We wouldn't be able to find him in this fog. Without a life preserver, he's already dead. Let me have your name and cabin number, then you can go back to your quarters. Tomorrow I'll come by and get a sworn statement. You get a good night's sleep and try not to think about it. You going to be okay?"

"Yes, sir. It's not like I knew him or anything."

When Donny returned to his compartment everyone was up waiting for him. Maude hugged him as soon as he walked in. Terry said, "Son, Meghan told us what happened. Did you not know what kind of danger you were in? It could have easily been you falling into the sea instead of that man."

"I realize it now. I was caught up in the moment and he was hurting Meghan."

"Well, I'm proud of you. But next time get help."

"Dad, I've got to hide my book on the strolling deck. I told the ship's officer that I was up there to get it. I didn't mention Meghan."

CHAPTER 45—A FUNERAL AT SEA
The Atlantic, June 1909

Relations with Meghan improved. She and Donny became inseparable as Meghan now considered Donny her personal guardian. Donny relished his role of looking out for a new confidante and before long they knew secrets about each other no one else knew. Meghan even helped Maude keep the items in the compartment in an orderly state. Meghan and Maude gathered Norah's personal effects and stored them in their compartment because the ship's medical officer said Norah would remain in the ship's infirmary for the remainder of the trip and Norah's compartment had to be sanitized. Meghan visited her mother each day and felt depressed by her mother's condition. She moped around for an hour or so after each visit.

On the fifth day several passengers assembled and pooled their knowledge of the procedures to follow upon arrival. Several had letters from relatives telling of the ordeal. Soon each person in the group knew the questions asked, the sicknesses not allowed, the chalk marks and what they meant, and the con schemes used to rob them of their money. For several days they practiced reciting their answers, listened critically to the answers given by others, and peered over maps deciding to where in America they'd travel.

Maude soaked up all the knowledge she might need. Terry said only one of them needed to be the expert. He spent his time dreaming of having a regular job, eating each meal until he was full, and buying a radio. He wanted to provide other things for his family as well, but first the radio.

On the sixth day when Meghan visited her mother, the attending nurse said that her mother had had a particularly hard night. She said, "Honey, we almost lost her last night. At one point her heart stopped beating. The doctor massaged it until it started back up, then her respiration became erratic. He's asleep now since he stayed up with her most of the night. If she wakes while you're visiting, make your peace with her. The priest recited the last rites an hour ago."

Meghan cried. She didn't know what she'd do without her mother. She and her dad were so much alike that they argued most of the time they were together. She'd have to make the relationship work. There would soon be no safe haven for her other than with her dad.

Meghan wiped away the tears and went in to her mother. She sat holding her hand until the nurse came to say the doctor wanted to make an examination. He would then talk to Meghan in his office.

The doctor thought that Norah was on the brink of death and that almost certainly today would be her last. She was now unconscious. He said that the ship usually buried at sea any passengers who died. He asked if Norah was a Christian and suggested the ship's chaplain say a few words before her body, wrapped in white linen, was lowered over the side.

Meghan went to the cabin and asked to be left alone for a while. Terry, Maude, and Donny went to the promenade deck and awaited the inevitable. That evening they attended the service and everyone cried as Norah's body slid into the icy waters of the North Atlantic.

CHAPTER 46—ARRIVING IN AMERICA
New York Harbor, June 1909

The SS *Celtic* arrived in New York during the afternoon of the eighth day. It was Wednesday, June 10, 1909. She dropped anchor outside New York Harbor at the lower quarantine station and waited for the medical inspectors to process the first and second class passengers. On the third class promenade deck, passengers gathered against the railing. They had tears in their eyes as the setting sun illuminated the land of their dreams. Here they would find jobs, establish families, grow rich and prosper. Here they would find happiness.

Aboard ship, the people leaning against the rail immediately went below decks and formed lines to bathe. With time off for the evening meal and a little frivolity it would be midnight before everyone desiring to present themselves the next day in the best possible condition was able to do so. Terry and Donny got into line at the same time as Maude and Meghan. After three hours the two boys were close to the washroom door and the two girls were still twenty feet away.

Terry said, "It appears the women dally when showering. On the average they must spend two minutes or more longer than us men."

"Maybe, Dad, the women have fewer shower stalls than the men or do a better job."

"Now that's an idea. Donny, when did you get to be so smart?"

"I don't know, Dad. It must've snuck up on me."

"What are you going to read after you finish Ivanhoe?"

"I thought I'd start The Last of the Mohicans. Do you have another you'd suggest?"

"No. That's an appropriate book. You might get an appreciation of what this land was like when the settlers were pitted against the red man. Christopher Columbus called them Indians because he thought he had made it to the shores of India. He was trying to find a sea route to the Spice Islands without having to go around the southern tip of Africa. When the Ottoman Turks conquered Constantinople they renamed it Istanbul and closed the overland spice routes that passed through."

189

"Why was spice so important?"

"Because our diet is bland without spices to season it. The European craves black pepper."

"Dad, when did you get to be so smart?"

"In school. I paid attention in school."

It was the last night aboard ship and everyone wanted to make it memorable. That evening the ship prepared the best meal of the trip. It was like she had been holding back thinking they might get lost at sea and needed the extra stores to safely see her passengers through. After the wonderful meal, several people brought out musical instruments and an impromptu songfest raised everyone's spirits to a feverish high. Maude started telling people that Terry was a singer of Irish ballads and soon people were yelling his name and clapping in unison.

After a particularly dreadful performance by someone a little too soused to stay in key Terry was coaxed to a make-shift stage. He took his harmonica out of its velvet pouch and, with the rapturous attention of everyone present, sang the first of several songs about the Emerald Isles. Homesick people cried. When he finished the first, he started to put the harmonica away, but his audience would have none of that and he had to sing a second, then a third. After a fourth he said he didn't know anymore and, to the dismay of everyone there, actually put his harmonica back in its velvet sack.

When he sat beside Maude and Donny his back was sore from being slapped so many times by adoring fans. Donny asked, "Dad, would you teach me to sing?" Donny was already shifting from being a private eye, with all its attendant danger, to a singer on the radio of Irish lullabies for swooning young ladies.

The next morning stewards brought boxes of cards—one for each passenger. Each card contained a passenger's name and where he or she was listed by page and line number on the ship's manifest. Maude looked through the box marked with a large "O" and found her family's cards. Each card also had a safety pin attached so it could be fastened to each passenger's shirt or blouse. They would need these cards for the legal part of the processing.

While everyone ate the morning meal and after the cards had been distributed, the SS *Celtic* weighed anchor. She soon steamed to a docking station on the southern point of Manhattan Island. On the way she passed the Statue of Liberty. The immigrants grew quiet as the ship slipped by this colossal centennial present from the people of France. They had given it to commemorate the friendship of the two nations. It was a solemn moment and one the passengers would remember for the rest of their lives.

After docking, the third class passengers stood at the railing with the baggage they planned on carrying and marveled at the huge skyscrapers planted at their feet. Gangplanks were lowered and people started walking down the passageway.

"Mom, do we get off here?"

"Yes, Donny. But we have to wait for the first and second class passengers to get off first. The baggage we can't carry will transfer to a ferry and then we'll get off. Several ferries are standing by to haul us to Ellis Island. That's where we'll be processed. I think it's time for us to make our way. Do you want to ask Meghan to walk with us?"

Meghan stood to one side. She had been quiet all morning. Last night she had gone through her mother's luggage looking for mementos. The clothing was delivered to the medical officer for incineration and the items she had decided to keep were placed back in the suitcase along with her clothes. The sack was trashed. It was a sad event and broke Maude's heart to watch.

By eleven o'clock on the morning of June 11, 1909, the first trip carrying third class passengers made its way to Ellis Island.

CHAPTER 47—ELLIS ISLAND
Near the New Jersey shore, June 1909

Three ferries, making several trips each, transported the third class passengers to Ellis Island. The O'Reillys, with Meghan tagging along, came over on the second series of trips. They arrived at noon and were welcomed by a beautiful main building. A large awning covered the walkway from the building's entrance to the ferry dock. Terry figured the building was at least 200 feet wide and 60 to 70 feet high. Groups of immigrants congregated outside according to their language. Interpreters were assigned to make sure they were processed properly.

Donny reached for Meghan's hand and led his family and Meghan inside the main building. Meghan was overcome with emotion and clutched hard the charitable hand. She looked around for her father. Maude said, "Does your father know when you were to arrive?"

"Mom sent him a letter the day we purchased our tickets. In it she told him the name of the ship. I suppose he could find out from the White Star office the day they expected us."

Terry said, "This way. They want us to check our luggage first then climb the grand staircase to the second floor. That's where we'll get our physical inspection."

Seated at a desk with a good view of the staircase was a doctor. It was his job to observe the immigrants as they ascended the staircase. A series of signals was sent to an aide at the top of the stairs. He held a stick of chalk and occasionally stopped an immigrant to mark something on his shirt.

On the second floor Terry led his entourage to the Registry Room. They were asked questions, prodded with sticks, had their eyelids pulled back, received vaccinations, and had their eyesight and hearing checked. Sometimes an immigrant received one or more chalk marks. A different letter for each problem: back, heart, lameness, heavy breathing, or a mental condition. If the letter was circled then the inspector had made a notification that he suspected a severe case. Each immigrant with a chalk mark was detained for further scrutiny.

Terry, Maude, Donny, and Meghan passed through the physical examinations without the slightest bit of difficulty. They moved to the legal test with the "primary" line inspector. A man sat at a desk. From the card attached to the front of their clothing he looked up their answers to the twenty-nine questions. It was his job to ascertain the correctness of the immigrant's answers and decide whether an immigrant was "clearly and beyond a doubt entitled to land." He did his work at a clip of no more than two minutes per immigrant.

Donny and Meghan were asked to read a line of scripture. Terry was asked how much money he carried and Maude was asked if she was capable of accomplishing work. Receiving satisfactory answers they were given landing cards and told to go to the money exchange.

At the money exchange a blackboard listed the exchange rate for gold, silver, and paper currency from numerous countries. Terry and Meghan stepped forward and put their money in a tray for the cashier to count and translate into dollars according to the posted rate.

Maude noticed several people left carrying small paper sacks. She asked a woman she had met on the trip what the sack was for.

"Honey, it's a sack lunch. They're free and available in the cafeteria. I'm headed to catch a ferry to New Jersey. I've already purchased train tickets from there to St. Louis. Is this not a wonderful place?"

"Maude, I know we thought we'd stay in New York City, but I'm now thinking Boston. From what I've heard there are a lot of Irish in New York City. In Boston there are just as many and the city offers a warmer welcome."

Maude reached into her purse for the list of mail she had to deliver. "I got fifteen names in New York City and ten, twelve, fifteen . . . I got eighteen names for Boston."

"Meghan, where does your dad live?" Maude stuffed the list back into her purse.

"In the Bowery. It's a neighborhood in south Manhattan."

"Have you thought how you would get in touch with him if he doesn't show to pick you up?"

"I have an address, but he hasn't written any letters for the last six months."

Terry wrapped his money in a ball and encircled it with a rubber band before stuffing it in a pocket. "They won't let you leave on your own. You'll have to wait here till he comes for you. I understand they have overnight accommodations and the food is free. However, you're welcome to come with us."

"I'll be all right, Mr. O'Reilly. Really, I will."

The four travelers went to the railway ticket booth and purchased three tickets for Boston. They were shown a place to wait for a ferry to carry them to Jersey City. Their train left in two hours. Terry determined where Meghan's father would most likely arrive to pick Meghan up and pointed to the most convenient spot for her to wait.

"Meghan, it might be a day or two."

"I know, but the people are friendly. I've already been asked if I will need lodging, and I know where the cafeteria and washroom facilities are. I'll be just fine."

When the ferry started boarding for Jersey City, Terry put his arm around Meghan and said, "Good luck. If you ever get to Boston look us up."

Maude sniffled as she said, "Meghan, honey, you are one brave girl. All alone in this god-awful big place. I worry for you. Won't you please come with us? You can write to your dad and he can pick you up in Boston. Or we'll bring you back ourselves."

"That's kind of you, Mrs. O'Reilly, but he'll be here any minute and you don't want to miss your train." The two women hugged. Meghan looked down at Donny who shuffled his feet. She kissed him on his forehead and said, "I will miss you most of all." She put both arms around Donny and said, "You are my hero, my knight. You are Ivanhoe."

Meghan stuffed a folded piece of paper into his shirt pocket with her father's address. "Write to me, Ivanhoe."

CHAPTER 48—BOSTON
Boston, December 1914

On the ferry to the Jersey shore Donny asked his dad if he thought Meghan would be all right. His dad assured him she would, but Donny persisted. Then he worked on his mother. When they landed his dad purchased return tickets and they went back after Meghan. When they arrived at Ellis Island, Meghan was gone and no one could remember anyone coming from Manhattan Island for a young girl.

Donny wrote his first letter on the train to Boston. A month later, he got a reply from Meghan saying she had left soon after Donny and his parents had boarded the ferry. She had purchased her own ticket and left tagging along the fringes of another departing family. She found her dad living in a run-down tenement building. He didn't have a job, there were no groceries and no electricity. Donny learned she eventually got a job as a waitress in one of the diner's inside a drug store and became the means of support for her drunken father. Over the years Donny wrote long letters to Meghan about every other month. Meghan was not good about replying but did send a birthday card every year and the occasional short note.

Then the week before Christmas five and a half years after first falling in love, Donny got a one-sentence letter that said. "Help me, Ivanhoe."

Donny sold his bicycle and a set of weights he kept in a storage shed. He left that afternoon for New York City. Donny was seventeen. He had an address and almost a hundred dollars in his pocket. He left a note for his mother and the message he'd received from Meghan.

When Donny knocked on Meghan's door, no one answered. Thinking she was probably at work, he left to get lunch. He'd spend the day waiting; he'd wait forever if need be.

A shoe-shine stand stood at the intersection of one of the avenues and the side street where he had found Meghan's address. A black man had two chairs on pedestals for his customers and another for himself where he sat between customers. Donny said, "Do you mind if I sit in one of the chairs? I'm waiting for a friend."

"How long you be?"

"Not long, but how about letting me rent the chair?"

"I can see that."

Donny reached into his pocket. "I'll pay you fifty cents an hour or two dollars for the rest of the day. Your choice." Donny held up two dollar bills.

The black man said, "I'm good," and snatched both bills.

The rest of the afternoon Donny observed the day-to-day routines in the neighborhood: boys threw a football in the street, residents sat on their front stoops watching other people and talking, and pedestrians walked aimlessly by with no place to be. No one entered or came out of the falling-down building he had been mailing his letters to. An hour before dark the black man said, "Mister, I'm calling it a day. Your friend ain't gonna show. You're welcome to wait as long as you want, just cover the chair with this sheet when you leave."

"Thanks. Have a merry Christmas."

With the dark approaching a chill descended and Donny thought about shelter. Then a single female figure approached. She walked by the stand with her head down, hands deep in her pockets, and continued down the side street.

Donny jumped from the chair and ran toward the slow-moving creature. "Is that you, Meghan?"

The woman looked up and smiled. "No, but I could be. You need to ward off the cold? I could keep you warm, dearie."

"Uh, no. I thought you were the person I've been waiting for."

"Ivanhoe. Oh, Ivanhoe. You did come." A second woman ran up and put her arms around Donny. The first woman lowered her gaze and continued her slow walk.

"I've been here a while. Knocked on your door and then waited with the shine guy. I was worried you'd moved. Can we go inside? I'm shivering."

"No, we can't go inside. There's an all-night diner around the corner and down a block. Let's go there. Something warm does sound good."

The diner was about half full. Donny took off his coat and hung it on a hook by the front door. Meghan said she'd keep hers on.

"So tell me how you and your family have fared," said Meghan.

"Dad got a job with the police department, and Mom stayed home with me. Then Dad tried to break up a fight and a man pulled a knife. Dad was stabbed. They took him to the hospital. Mom said he wasn't going back, she'd mop floors if she had to, but he was not going to such a dangerous job. When he got out of the hospital Mom made good her threat. She had started a pie business called Maude's Splendid Pies. Mom's got good business sense. We were selling a dozen pies a day when Dad came home. He and I now deliver to about half of the restaurants in Boston. How about you?"

"I've already told you almost everything in my letters."

"Would that be the first one or the second?"

"Donny, I wrote you more than two."

"Okay. But what's going on now?"

Meghan removed her hat and muffler. There were red welts on her neck and purple places tinged in yellow under one eye. They extended from her cheek to under her left ear. "My father can't find a job so he sits around the house all day drinking. It takes everything I can make to keep him in liquor. Sometimes he gets upset and hits me. Then I have to work in the kitchen. I can't make as much money there as waiting tables so he hits me more when my wages go down. Donny, I have to leave town."

"Get your things. I'll take you to Boston."

"I'm nineteen. I can't live in your house."

"Meghan, go get your things. We'll let Mom and Dad figure something out."

"If you're sure, then I need to stay one more night. There are some of Mother's things I need to get and a few clothes for me. I'll set them out after he goes to sleep. Tomorrow I'll work and tell them it'll be my last day. I can't simply not show. They've been good to me. We'll leave tomorrow after I help serve the evening meal."

"Okay. Where can I meet you?"

"Here. We'll eat before we leave. Now I've got to go or he'll beat me for staying out too late."

"I could have a talk with him."

"I know you would, Donny, but he's only a miserable old man. When I don't come home and he can't find me he'll have to give up the bottle and get a job. It's that or starve. Sometimes you have to quit making it easy for that kind of person."

After walking Meghan back to her place Donny headed to a more prosperous area where he could secure lodging for the night. The next day he checked the train schedule to Boston and found that the latest would leave too early so he paid for an additional night's lodging and spent the rest of the day exploring the streets of New York City.

At five in the evening it was getting dark as he continued to wait for Meghan at the diner. She came in bringing the suitcase he'd seen her drag around Ellis Island. "Meghan, have a seat. Would you like something warm to drink?"

"Tea, if they have it."

Donny ordered hot tea and handed Meghan a menu. "We have to stay the night. The latest train to Boston left two hours ago." Meghan looked over the top of the menu at Donny. He said, "Don't worry. I made them bring an extra blanket. I'll sleep on the floor."

"When we get to your parent's place we're not going to mention spending the night together. Are you with me on this?"

"Absolutely."

At the hotel the elevator was turned off so they walked up three flights of stairs. On the way Meghan asked, "Do they have hot water?"

"Yeah—but not in the room. There are two washrooms on each floor. They got towels, but you have to supply your own soap. You can use mine."

"Do you have a toothbrush too? When I wore mine out, I didn't have money to replace it. My clothes are rags. I haven't purchased anything for myself since . . . since I can't remember when."

When they reached the third floor and walked down a dimly lit corridor Donny said, "Tomorrow before we leave we'll buy you some new clothes. Not too much though. I don't have a sack full of money, but I think I can squeeze out enough for a couple of dresses and a pair of shoes."

"And underwear?"

"Actually, I like my women almost naked."

200

"Ha, ha." Meghan lowered her head. Tears rolled down her cheek. Donny sat her suitcase down by the radiator and handed her his handkerchief. "I'm sorry, Donny. That's the first time I've laughed in ages. I almost didn't recognize the emotion."

After surveying the room Meghan said she was really looking forward to bathing and asked Donny for the soap. While Meghan was out of the room Donny pulled back her covers and fixed himself a pallet at the foot of the bed. Meghan returned wrapped in a towel.

"If I was to cut holes for my arms and stick on a couple of buttons you could save some of that money."

"Nonsense. White isn't the color of choice this late in the season."

"Oh, Donny, it feels so good to laugh." She reached out, putting both arms around his shoulders she hugged him tight. "You're just like a little brother."

Donny was crushed. He headed down the hall with a change of underwear and a deflated ego. When he returned Meghan was sound asleep and all the lights were out. He felt his way to the pallet and crawled in. Around midnight the hotel turned off the steam and the room started cooling down. In an hour Donny was shivering.

"If you'll behave you can get in bed."

With his teeth chattering Donny said, "I'll do anything."

"Donny, the right answer is 'I'll not do anything.'"

"All right, that too."

When they arrived in Boston Donny had barely enough money for a taxi. Soon Meghan was hugging Maude and Terry was thinking about where to put her as Donny loaded the delivery truck with his mother's pies.

"Mom, I thought Meghan could help you bake the pies. You've been talking about expanding."

"She could, but it's hot work. Maybe your dad could buy us another fan."

Terry walked over and put his arm around Meghan. "Or maybe he could move you into larger quarters with a commercial oven or two and long stainless steel tables for decorating and packaging the pies."

"Now that would be the ticket."

For the next year Meghan lived upstairs over Maude's new place of business. She helped Maude bake and, on occasion, helped Terry make deliveries. There were even times when Donny visited. His parents thought he was out with his friends, but it was only one friend he was interested in being with.

One day Meghan said, "Donny, there's something I have to tell you."

"Is this something really serious?"

"Yes, it is. Donny, I'm going to marry Curtis."

"Meghan—no! I love you, Meghan. No one can take care of you like I can."

"Don't make this any harder than it has to be. Curtis and I have been seeing each other for a month and I've already met his parents. We'll have a brick house on a hill and I won't have to work. I can have whatever I want."

"Curtis? Is he the one who owns that fancy restaurant downtown?"

"Yes. I delivered pies to him and now he's proposed."

"Just like that?"

"Yep. Says he loves me. He took me sailing on his boat last weekend." Meghan put her arm around Donny. "Be happy for me, Ivanhoe."

After the wedding Donny told his mother he had been talking with the priest. "They're making arrangements for me to enter seminary."

"Oh, Donny. I am so proud. You always said you wanted to be a priest."

Terry shook Donny's hand and then gave him a hug. He turned to Maude, "Honey, the biggest part of your workforce is leaving. Meghan got married and now, a week later, Donny says he's going into the church." Terry abruptly let loose of his son, backed off a few steps and gave a new appraisal. "Are you sure this is what you want? Not decided on because something else didn't work out?"

"Yes, Dad. This is what I want to do."

"It's a surprise to me. I didn't think you were so religiously inclined."

"Leave the boy alone, Terry. I've known about it for years."

PART III
THE GREAT DEBATE

CHAPTER 49—THREE SHEETS TO THE WIND
Dancing Deer, Arkansas, March 1944

Spring in northern Arkansas is particularly beautiful. It's the time of year when jonquils, hyacinths, and tulips poke their heads above ground and dot the landscape. It's the time of year when farmers prepare their fields and their wives' gardens for the upcoming growing season. They turn rows, pull and burn stumps, and mend fences. It's the time of year when impregnated cows give birth to a new generation of table fare.

How does the saying go? "March winds bring April showers for May flowers." Heck thought about the rhyming sentence over again and decided he should pay more attention to the literature that interested his children. You can't simply cohabit a house and be oblivious to the areas of interest of the others living with you. May would know the proper wording. He'd get her to teach it to him.

When Heck reached his house he paused while he deciphered the information before him. Someone was visiting. A black Hudson sedan sat on the driveway. He didn't know anyone who drove such an automobile. He surveyed the area to see what else might be different. The tire swing was missing; a stack of lumber sat in the grass beside his storage shed; his grove of pine trees had their bases painted white and wrapped in chicken wire; and new curtains replaced his venetian blinds. What has gotten into Janice?

Heck opened the front door and walked inside. New furniture decorated his living room. "Janice, I'm home. Otis? May? Anyone here?" Heck walked to the kitchen. He could hear a radio playing. Someone was here.

When he entered the kitchen he saw her. Janice was bent over placing something on the bottom rack of her oven. She raised and turned around—and screamed.

"I'm sorry, Miss. Uh, what are you doing in my house?"

The woman screamed again. She pulled out a large kitchen knife from a wooden block. "Don't you come near me. My husband will be here any minute."

"Where's my wife? My kids?"

The woman held the knife in front with the blade at waist level. She slowly slid sideways. "Don't move, I'm going to call the police."

"Ma'am, that won't be necessary. I'll leave if you'll answer a question or two."

The woman paused and waited.

"How long have you lived here?"

"Two months."

"Two months? Are you sure? What's today's date?"

"Yes, I'm sure. Today is the 16th of March, 1944. Thursday."

Heck had to think. He thought he'd only been gone a few weeks, two months tops, but this lady just told him he'd been in the woods for almost five months. No wonder his family moved on. They must've thought he'd died out there—eaten by bears or mountain lions or drowned in the river. "Okay. What happened to the previous residents?"

"I don't know. The house was vacant when we moved in."

"No furniture? No children's toys?"

"No."

Heck turned to go. "I'm sorry to have scared you. I haven't been myself lately." He walked out the front door, down the sidewalk to the street, and turned toward town. When he passed the shed, he stole behind it and continued through a grove of evergreens to the tree house he'd built for Otis. Heck located a hidden cord and pulled down a rope ladder. When he had ascended around twelve feet he switched to the steps he'd nailed to the tree and pulled the rope ladder back up into its hiding place. The makeshift cabin was another ten feet higher. Sticking his head through the trap door, Heck realized his family had indeed left. All of Otis's things he played with in his hideout were gone. Heck sat on the floor to think.

In a few minutes a police car drove up. Heck raised a shutter flap and placed a stick into a notch to hold it open. He could see the back and side of his house along with part of the driveway. Two men wearing navy-blue uniforms walked to the house from their cruiser. Soon they came out and left in the direction he'd walked when leaving an hour earlier.

How could he have been gone so long? Heck remembered his wife coming home from work and finding him passed out on the sofa. He'd spent the day getting rid of a mason jar of moonshine. She told him that he had better sleep in the shed, that she didn't want the kids to see him that way. That evening he ate with Otis's spaniel, Curley. The next day he'd finished the jar. He and Curley became close friends, but Heck knew neither was welcome in the house. Janice brought a second plate of food on the second evening and said that when he sobered up and planned on staying that way, he could come back in.

Those two days saw a stream of people come by his house and knock on his door. He kept hid in the shed. Most of the visitors he didn't know anyway. A few were students. He didn't feel like talking to anyone. When Janice brought his meal in the evening of the second day, Heck said he might go on a camp-out for a couple of days. He rounded up the tent, sleeping bag, and a few other useful items he had taken when camping overnight with Otis's Boy Scout troop. His wife supplied a sack of food and he tried to kiss her good-bye, but she wouldn't let him, saying he smelled bad and his clothes reeked of alcohol.

During the time he'd been away he'd found a field of rabbit tobacco, fished in the Big Piney River, figured out how to start a fire with a piece of flint, and explored the woods right out his backdoor.

One day a black cloud gathered on the horizon and Heck wondered how his flimsy tent would hold up if a gully-washer unleashed its forces. He decided to find more secure lodging. On one of the scouting expeditions Otis had uncovered a cave on a cliff face. Heck made the cave his new home. He built a fire in the entrance and cleared the floor of rubble. With a hand-ax, he gathered wood to stack in a corner of his new home.

In the evening, the clouds burst and rain pelted down in sheets. Puddles of water gathered in the cave entrance and the wind blew tiny droplets into its recesses. Heck took a stick and dug channels in the cave floor to link the puddles together then a deeper channel out to a slope. In a matter of minutes the accumulated water drained away. He added fuel to the fire and sat on his flattened tent. How long would he have to wait?

Heck knew his wife would let him back into the house if he was sober. It wasn't like he was a drunk or anything. He just wanted people to leave him alone. How long before they forgot Coach Jolly's infamous accusation? How long before life could return to normal?

Heck lived on wild berries and fish from the river. Occasionally he added a rabbit he snared in a trap. His drinking water poured out of springs or cracks in the rocks on cliff faces and rushed to the river. Heck filled his canteen every morning. All in all Heck had made himself fairly comfortable.

CHAPTER 50—A STRANGER IN OUR MIDST
Dancing Deer, Arkansas, March 1944

Heck descended the ladder. He had to find his family. From the shed he retrieved another mason jar of moonshine and counted the remaining jars in a cardboard box at the far reaches of a high shelf. Ten more jars. There was probably a story of how they had been placed there but he had no way of finding it out. Heck stuffed the jar in his knapsack with his tent and sleeping bag.

On the sidewalk people moved out of his way. People just weeks earlier, or months if the lady was correct, who knew his name. Back then they asked how he was doing. Now they looked the other way or nodded and kept walking.

Were they so consumed with hatred for someone with a different set of beliefs or did they not recognize him? Heck thought about his appearance. He had lost seventy-five pounds or more. His hair was down past his shoulders and facial hair covered everything but his eyes. His clothes were also pretty much a disguise. His shoes were without laces. Both shoes had holes in their soles. His pants and shirt were several sizes too large, just hanging on his skinny frame. New notches cut in his belt now cinched up his pants so he wouldn't have to walk around using one hand to hold them up. Heck reconsidered. No one recognized him. He had become the town vagrant—the one nobody wanted to admit was in their midst.

Heck needed to eat. He didn't have any money. A handout was his only alternative. He walked to the Baptist church his wife attended and found the doors locked. He didn't know where the minister lived so decided to try another church. It was also locked. Would he have to wait until Sunday? When he walked past the Catholic church, he heard children playing on the other side of a rock wall. Heck opened a wooden gate to the playground area and sat on a bench watching them play.

A tall man in a frock coat walked to him. "Good morning. Have you eaten today?"

"No." Heck had expected Father O'Reilly to recognize him.

211

"Follow me. I'll take you to the kitchen. Someone should be putting away stuff from our noon meal."

"That's kind of you, father."

"Think nothing of it. The church is here for everyone." The father extended his hand. "I'm Father Donovan O'Reilly."

Heck stood and shook Father Don's hand saying, "I appreciate your offer. I'm—my name is—uh, Cody. My name is Cody."

"Pleased to meet you, Cody. This way."

Heck sat down in a corner of the church's kitchen. Another priest entered, filled a cup with coffee, nodded to Heck, and stepped into the hallway with Father O'Reilly. Heck wondered how he could find out where his family was without giving up his hidden identity.

After eating Heck went looking for Father O'Reilly. He found him at the entrance to the playground. "Father, is there anything I can do to repay you for the meal?"

"That's not necessary, Cody. The church doesn't require repayment for its kindnesses."

"That's fine, but I want to. I've always paid my way."

"Interesting. You don't accept charity when it's freely given? Sometimes repayment is made just by being receptive to another's generosity. There's a wonderful feeling that comes over a charitable person who's able to help a person in need. If you have to repay, then that feeling loses a portion of its luster. If you insist, you may pull weeds in the church's cemetery."

"I'd like that. Maybe you could look at it not as any kind of repayment, but as a charitable act in itself."

"Fair enough."

For the rest of the afternoon Heck did the best he could at ridding the Dancing Deer Catholic Cemetery of unwanted vegetation. He had to pace his work so that he didn't wear himself out or complete his work before the priest made his way back after classes were over. Heck still needed answers.

Two hours later the priest tapped Heck on his shoulder and held out a glass of iced tea. "You've got quite a pile there, Cody."

"Yes, sir. Do you happen to have a hoe?" Heck had both hands throttling a particularly troublesome weed. "Last time I was in town I

212

helped a man down the street plant some pine trees. Today someone else lives in his house and they said they didn't have any work for me. I guess the man moved. Do you know where he went? I think he worked at the school."

"You must be talking about Mr. Stout. I haven't seen him for months. I heard he left to find another teaching job. When he found it he sent for his family."

"Uh, do you remember who told you that? Maybe they know where he moved. I owe him some money and I'd love to pay it back. I don't come by money often and if I don't send it soon, I'm afraid I'll spend it."

"A Mrs. Wheeler told me."

"I'm sorry I don't know a Mrs. Wheeler."

"Cody, where are you staying? I'll tell Mrs. Wheeler you need to talk with her."

"I could finish the cemetery tomorrow. Maybe I could talk to her here? I only need a minute."

"Cody, Mrs. Wheeler teaches first grade at the public elementary school. She couldn't come by before tomorrow afternoon. I could ask your questions for you. Do you just need to know where Mr. Stout and his family now reside?"

"That's it."

"Come eat lunch with me tomorrow and I'll find out what she knows."

"You've got a deal. Is there a place I can wash my hands? And where would you like me to put this pile?"

"We have a compost bin. You can put it there. A water hydrant is close to it, but the water's cold. Why don't you wash in the bathroom down the hall from the kitchen? I'll make sure there's soap."

CHAPTER 51—CODY
Dancing Deer, Arkansas, March 1944

Early the next morning, Heck descended from the treehouse and walked through the woods to a tributary of the Big Piney River. In a secluded spot, he removed his clothing and washed. He had used his knife to cut the bar of soap in half at the church and used his half to wash. The water was mighty cold and Heck had a difficult time staying in long enough to get his hair done as well as his body. When he climbed out of the water he didn't have anything to dry with. He shook like Otis's dog, wrung out his hair and wrapped it in his underwear. For the rest of his body, he used his hand like a window cleaner scrapes off excess water. His efforts were only partially effective so he put on his clothes over a damp and cold body.

Without a comb Heck's hair dried haphazardly. He ran his hands through trying to make it lay down. He felt he should get out of the woods at his first convenience—otherwise he might get shot by a hunter thinking he'd run across some new upright predator.

On the way to the church, people stopped to look at the hideous creature ambulating down the sidewalk. Children hid in their mother's skirts. Men gave plenty of room and women stepped off the sidewalk looking for someone to talk to. When Heck got to the Catholic church, he walked around to the back and knocked on the door to the kitchen. The cook opened the door and gasped. She put her hand to her mouth, then let out a cackle as she finally understood the vagrant had washed his mop of hair and it now extended in all directions.

"Come in, Cody. Did you scare any children?"

"Yes ma'am, I left a trail of them along the way."

"Have a seat and sip this cup of coffee. I'll get Father O'Reilly."

Heck and Father O'Reilly shook hands, the priest blessed the food, and the two ate. Heck noticed the priest smiled when he first came into the room but didn't say anything; he must've found the new hairstyle comical. Heck placed his napkin on his lap. He said, "I'm sorry for making such an unattractive appearance."

215

"Would you like for me to trim your hair? We also have baskets of used clothing. Most of it's for women, but I think we could find several items that would fit you. Do you need shoes?"

"Yeah, I only have what I have on. But don't you have to teach the orphans today?"

"You know I teach the orphans?"

"Uh—I made an educated guess."

"No. Today is Saturday. I gave each a dime and sent them to Eudy's. They'll use an hour figuring out the best way to spend their dime. Some will go to the library and others will come back here to play on the playground."

"Have you had a chance to talk with Mrs. Wheeler?"

"Yes. I'm sorry to say she doesn't know. She was the daughter's teacher. One day the little girl said she was moving. When Mrs. Wheeler asked where she was moving to the little girl didn't know. She started crying."

"Would you mind calling Mr. Blanchard? He was the teacher for the little boy."

"I already have. He didn't know either. He said he put the boy down as absent, and the elementary principal sent a note back saying the boy's mother had checked him out after school the day before without saying where they were moving."

"Another dead end."

"I'm afraid so. Are you ready for me to trim your locks? You can't go around looking like you belong in a circus. If you plan on staying for any length of time people will gradually accept you. But not at first with your appearance."

When Heck left that afternoon he wore a pair of overalls, a new cotton shirt, a leather jacket two sizes too large, and a pair of work boots that covered his ankles. He carried a sack with two similar outfits and additional underwear. He decided that he needed to find work so he headed downtown to see what was available.

Mr. Creighton said he'd give a dollar for someone to wash his store windows and another fifty cents to sweep the sidewalk in front. The city sanitation department said he could ride on the wagon they used every Monday morning to pick up the city's trash. A landfill was just outside of town and he could make four dollars if he helped pick up the trash and drop it off. The Livery Feed and Seed offered to let him muck-out stables. The Ritz Hotel Bistro offered to let him wash dishes. Part of his pay there would be a free meal.

If he wanted to find out what happened to his family this was the place to start. Tomorrow he would clean Mr. Creighton's windows then head to the Bistro. If he didn't give away his superior intelligence and didn't ask too many questions about the Stout family, his deception would probably not be compromised. He could keep it up until he had the information he needed.

Over the course of the next two weeks he talked to his old landlord, who apologized for supplying shelter to an atheist. He talked to the manager of the Livery Feed and Seed. Janice's old boss said she came in and told him she would work until the end of the week. She left town right after getting her last paycheck. The Reverend Mr. Colfax said Mrs. Stout attended church regularly. She brought the two children with her every Sunday after her husband ran off. When Heck asked the minister about the husband running away, the minister said that was his own supposition, that Mrs. Stout wouldn't talk to him about it. Heck called the bank and asked if a check he had from a Heck Stout was any good. He was informed the account had been closed for months. It was all dead-ends for Heck. He settled into a regular routine of doing odd jobs for the town's residents and civic jobs for the town itself—without pay whenever possible. Heck averaged two days a week picking up the town's litter. He improved his efficiency when he started using a long stick ending in a nail.

His favorite work was washing dishes at the Ritz Hotel Bistro. The kitchen was completely stainless steel. Someone had arranged the work space into several different cooking stations and three men worked at a quick pace hardly uttering a word. They were a marvel to watch. Before long Heck considered himself an integral part of the team. He was offered a full-time job, but Heck informed Andre—the Cajun chef in charge—that he wanted to work only enough to pay for his meals.

When Heck had earned an extra dollar or two he used it to buy the supplies he needed. He bought a stiff-bristled push broom he used to sweep the city's streets, leather gloves for hauling the trash on Monday, and an old bicycle he rode to the bridge over the Illinois Bayou. He bathed there several times a week and fitted together rocks and concrete rubble under the bridge to make a hidden cavern he used as a second place of refuge. He bought several tarps and lined the inside of his rock quarry to keep out drafts. Small animals were sometimes a problem, but he soon come to the opinion that if they did him no harm he would reciprocate.

Soon everyone in town knew they were the beneficiaries of an eccentric town vagrant and they sought him out when needing odd jobs done. One day Heck found an old top-hat sitting atop the trash not far from the stage door of the Hotel Ritz Bistro and Grand Ballroom. He began sporting it around town. Heck reasoned it had been discarded by one of the vaudeville actors that occasionally performed in the ballroom. Heck liked playing the role of someone a little daft and considered the hat an integral part of his act. People were friendly and greeted him by his fictitious name as he worked to keep their city clean.

Pretty soon Heck could ask anybody anything without that person being the least bit interested in knowing why. Heck found out from his neighbors that a big black Kaiser automobile had pulled up to his house just days before his family left. On his family's last Friday it returned with a moving van. Heck's wife loaded the kids into their family sedan and left, following the Kaiser. The moving van was the tail-end of a twentieth century wagon-train heading west.

CHAPTER 52—DREAMS
January 1946

Father O'Reilly returned from the Arkansas Archdiocese in Little Rock. How could they have lost his papers? He had been a priest for almost thirty years and now the church doesn't need him, doesn't know he exists, and is not supplying him with any assigned work. A month earlier every orphan in his care had been adopted by a family in Dancing Deer. Some families adopted two if the orphans were related. All of his children were now attending public school. Father Donovan O'Reilly was not a happy man.

There were two other priests at Saint Bartholomew's and neither was willing to relinquish any assigned duties. So Father O'Reilly, with no orphans to shepherd, no opportunity for ministering to the faithful, holding Mass, or officiating at any ceremony, spent his days in solitude. Out of desperation he traveled to Little Rock to talk with his superiors, but they were at a complete loss as to who he was.

The Monday following his return he went to the hospital and sat with Edwin Stankey. "Edwin, can you hear me?"

Edwin blinked one time, meaning yes.

"I don't understand. Do you think God is trying to tell me something?"

Edwin blinked.

"You need to get better, Edwin. I think you have a better grip on this than I. If God is trying to tell me something, along what lines might it be? Should I go back to Boston and check on my parents? Do I transfer to one of the large orphanages in St Louis or Chicago? Maybe I should write a book. A treatise on something spiritual? Synthesize aspects of secularization and spiritualism? But that doesn't sound like something I'd enjoy even if I was divinely inspired."

Gladys walked into the room and put her hand on Father O'Reilly's shoulder. "Doesn't Eddy look good?" She walked over and kissed her husband's forehead. "The doctor says he might go home

219

soon. The bank's buying him a hospital bed and will pay for someone to come during the daytime to help take care of him."

"I think that's great, Gladys. It always feels good to be needed. I'm going down the hall now to see if I can be of benefit to other patients. Let me know if I can be of any help. Any help at all."

"Thank you, Father, but I think we'll be all right."

That night Father O'Reilly had a fitful night. He dreamed of his youth, of falling in love, of killing a man, and of being told to talk to Cody. He tossed and turned, trying to repress memories in his subconscious. Why did he need to talk with Cody? When he woke, all he remembered was that he should visit the only other person in town without a job or a family.

Heck sat in his rock quarry home with his back against a piece of plywood he used as a side wall. Light flickered from a broken lantern he had salvaged and repaired. Turning a page in a book, he continued to read. Now that he had a library card, his evenings were not so long or uneventful as before. He checked out three or four books each week. Always one was on philosophy. The remaining books were only a cover so that the woman who marked his card would not be overly suspicious. Still, she must wonder why a man who rode a bicycle, wore a top hat, and spent his time sweeping streets would spend time struggling through a book by Schopenhauer or Husserl or Kant.

Heck closed his book, turned out the lantern, and fell into a deep sleep. In a vivid dream, the devil appeared and told him a plum was available for the picking. Father Donovan O'Reilly was wavering. Heck had to talk with him, convince him that the church didn't want him anymore, that he wasn't appreciated, wasn't needed. Religion was all bunk anyway. Heck resisted.

The devil said he could have his family back if he turned the cleric.

CHAPTER 53—FIRST SESSION
January 1946

The last Monday in January the wind whipped up flurries of snow. Heck Stout lay on a patched air mattress under several thick blankets supplied by Father O'Reilly. He had a white cotton sock stretched out of shape and pulled over his head down past his ears. Heck shuddered. It was cold. Bad weather had blown in during the night and his rock quarry didn't have a heater. Today he would ride the trash wagon and earn four dollars. Heck shivered and determined he'd use that money to buy a tent heater and a five-gallon container of kerosene from Eberly's Sporting Goods. It would definitely be a wise purchase.

Heck forced himself up. The wagon wouldn't wait and, now that he had figured a way to heat his home, he needed to make it happen. Heck put on two pairs of shorts and two shirts before sliding into his overalls. Leaving the top hat, he grabbed his bicycle and pushed it up the steep grade from under the bridge overpass to the county road. He was past the outskirts of town. It would take fifteen minutes of hard riding to get to the Livery Feed and Seed. When he arrived he thought he might be able to show a clean face with a little bit of work. His beard was frozen stiff so all he had to do was break it off. Heck shivered from his toes to the top of his head.

"Cody, I'm glad you showed up. No one else has made it." Aaron drove the wagon with two or sometimes three helpers hanging onto the back. The helpers dumped the trash in the wagon as Aaron slowly pulled it from house to house.

"They'll be here, Mr. Montgomery. The pay's too good and everyone has to eat."

Aaron adjusted the harness on Tony, the plow-horse Aaron had harnessed to the wagon. "We'll wait another fifteen minutes. If they're not here by then we'll head on out and they can catch up the best way they can."

"It'll be a long day if I'm the only one loading. Let's ask Tony if he wants to stay out in this weather for the entire day."

"Now, Cody, it won't be that bad. We'll only work until the wagon is full one time and do the rest tomorrow. That way you can earn twice what you normally make."

"I don't care about the money. Well, maybe this one time I might, but normally I don't."

"Climb aboard, Cody. It's time to go. You going to be warm enough—what's with that sock on your head?"

Around lunch, Heck finished unloading the wagon at the landfill and jumped on the buckboard seat beside Aaron for the return trip to town. "Mr. Montgomery, are you a religious man?"

"As much as the next guy. My wife drags me to church every Sunday. She says she doesn't want to get to heaven and find out I didn't make it."

"Would you be a religious man if your wife didn't coerce you?"

"Yeah, probably so. Everyone needs something to believe in. This can't be all there is. What's with you, Cody? I've never considered you as much of a questioning man, a man who didn't have it figured out or didn't care one way or the other."

"I'm just wondering why Dancing Deer has so many churches and why everyone in town attends one. I've been on occasion but never found the sermons to be much more than fluff. If a man is going to preach to me, I need to know where he gets his knowledge, why that knowledge is beyond reproach, and what gives him the right to do so in the first place."

"Cody, why don't you be a preacher? Your congregation would supply you with a furnished house to live in, transportation to visit your flock, and a small salary. For that you'd have to rant and rave for an hour each Sunday morning and for a half hour Sunday and Wednesday evenings. If you could learn to do magic tricks, sing, or play the piano or guitar, you might even get to take your act on the road or to one of the more wealthy churches paying better wages."

In the afternoon Cody purchased his stove and kerosene. Herman Eberly also sold him a basket for his bicycle that took both men a good thirty minutes to figure out how to install it. With the heater and kerosene tied to his new basket Heck headed to Saint Bartholomew's Holy Catholic Church. In Father O'Reilly's study, Heck sat in a comfortable chair by the fire. The cook supplied a generous cup of coffee and a plate of cookies and little sandwiches on toothpicks. Heck ate one after another as Father O'Reilly watched.

"Father Don, I'm perplexed. I was hoping you would answer some questions for me."

"Sure. What would you like to know, Cody?"

"Well, for one thing. If the Bible is the inspired word of God and if the church relies on it as the infallible guide by which she leads her minions, why are there so many mistakes in it?"

"What mistakes are you talking about?"

"Let's take the four Gospels. Matthew and Luke give different lineages for Joseph, different years and under different reigns for Jesus' birth, different ways of Joseph and Mary getting to Bethlehem, different scenarios after leaving Bethlehem, and different appearances of Jesus after his resurrection. Matthew said Jesus was born in a house and Luke says he was born in a manger.

"There are even differences within the same gospel. In Mark 6:44 the narrator says Jesus fed five thousand people with five loaves of bread and two fish. In Mark 8:9 four thousand were fed and this time there were seven loaves of bread.

"In the three synoptic Gospels, the last supper was the Passover meal, but in John it was held on the day before Passover.

"In Matthew, Mary Magdalene and the other Mary, I take her to be the mother of Jesus, were the first to arrive at the grave at dawn on the first day of the week. A single angel sat on the stone that had been barring entrance to the grave. Later these same two women were the first to see the risen Savior when they left the tomb and traveled the road to Galilee." Heck paused to take a sip of his coffee and to see if he could make anything out of Father O'Reilly's facial expression.

"In Mark no angel sat on the stone when they arrived, but inside the grave was a young man wearing a white robe. Mark says in chapter 16, verse 9, that Jesus first appeared to Mary Magdalene while she was alone on the road to Galilee.

"In Luke 24:4 two men, wearing dazzling apparel, suddenly stood near the many women inside the tomb. To the two Marys Luke adds Joanna. None of the others are named. The first sighting of the risen Jesus in Luke was to Cleopas and an un-named friend while they walked along the road to a village called Emmaus." Heck grabbed a little sandwich on a toothpick.

"In John, Mary Magdalene went alone to Jesus' tomb. His body was missing and no angel or young man was there to explain what had happened. She returned to inform Simon Peter. Peter and another disciple ran to the grave. They entered the tomb and found the linen wrappings, but no body and returned to their homes. Mary stayed and wept. She looked one last time in the tomb and beheld two angels in white. Also, Jesus made his first appearance to her while she was in the grave conversing with the two angels.

"So, Father Don, which one is right, and which ones are spurious? In what year was Jesus born? Was it during the reign of Herod or two years later at the time when Quirinius governed Syria? Did they travel to Bethlehem or were they already there? Was Jesus born in a manger or a house? What day did they eat the last supper? Who, if there was someone, accompanied Mary Magdalene at dawn to the tomb? Did they see one or two angels or were they men? Who did Jesus first reveal himself to? Was it Mary, Mary Magdalene and Mary, the mother of James, or was it to Cleopas?

"Father, these are not the only discrepancies. There are many others."

Father O'Reilly shook his head. "Cody, you are not the man you appear to be. Evidentially you have studied the Bible in great detail. And you have given these questions careful thought. I would be remiss if I spoke without giving my answer the same consideration. Please give me until tomorrow to research and properly phrase my reply.

"As a sort of appeasement I can say right now that the Bible does not err in what it conveys. It's man's interpretation that has the inconsistencies. We have to dig deeper to see exactly what God wants us to understand and not be put off by superficialities in the Bible that have little bearing on the real message."

"Okay, Father, but while you're figuring out how to answer those questions think about the wandering Jew, and why Jesus damned the fig tree."

CHAPTER 54—SECOND SESSION
January 1946

During his nights Heck had recurring nightmares. In one he heard his children cry. He ran down a dark corridor and opened a heavy door. From the last length of firm footing he peered into a black void. Two disembodied heads floated in the quiet darkness. May started crying. She said, "Daddy, save us. I'm scared."

The other face was Otis. He said, "Dad, this is the most awful place. Can you not turn the cleric?"

In another dream Janet screamed, "Heck, I've lost the children. I've lost the children." This was followed by uncontrolled sobbing then, "Heck, you've got to help us. I can't go on. Please, Heck. It's up to you now." Her voice and vision diminished as she spoke like she was being swept away through time and space. Heck ran to the image, but nothing—there was absolutely nothing. She was gone. In the dream he fell to his knees, sobbing.

Morning finally came, but Heck didn't want to get up. He tossed from one side to the other under his blankets. There was no safe place. Heck didn't remember much of his dreams. He only had a lingering fear for his family and a sense of urgency. He pulled the covers close around him as the wind howled. Foreboding seeped in like mustard gas seeking soldiers.

The tent-heater spewed and spit to warm his one-room palace. Heck couldn't force himself to climb out from under the voluminous covers. A black and white rat had snuck in and now sat behind a pile of books. It was not a day fit for man nor beast, but Heck knew Aaron and Tony would be waiting and he did not want to be thought of as a man who didn't keep his word. Repressing worry, Heck decided he would see the priest in the afternoon and make a more concerted effort.

More education was now required to become a priest. Besides going through seminary, the church required secular credentials. Father Donovan O'Reilly wondered if he could infuse ideas from the world's

225

literature outside the church into his reply to Cody's questions. Would he increase his ability to intelligently answer Cody if he'd read more history? More from the world's great non-Catholic books? He knew numerous scientists like Newton and Descartes had stepped from their laboratories to study certain aspects of faith. He was well versed in the religious sector, but secular writers were important too. He had been negligent in studying their efforts. Saint Bart's had a decent library and he immersed himself in its confines.

"Mrs. Wellington, would you bring a cup of hot tea to the library?"

"More than happy to. Did Cody give you a problem to solve?"

"Yes, he did. What do you know about it?"

"Just what Agnes told me. She and Father Dan overheard the two of you talking through the door."

"So why hasn't one of them offered to help me formulate the answers?"

"I don't think they want you to know they were listening."

Agnes Holloway was the church secretary, accountant, organizer, and main person behind the scenes. Saint Bartholomew operated efficiently mainly because of her ability to make everyone else toe the line. Father Dan was the most senior and the most possessive of his ministering tasks. Father William was the second in command and another not willing to share duties with a displaced Father O'Reilly.

"If you would be so kind as to let me know the next time someone listens to my confidential conversation with a parishioner, I'd bless you and your family."

"Sir, they told me to bring chairs—four of them—to the hallway outside your study when Cody gets here."

"And that would be chairs for Father Dan, Father William, Agnes, and . . ."

"And one for me."

"I see. You can forget the tea. Bring me strong coffee. If I'm going to have such an impressive audience, I had better do a good job."

In the afternoon Agnes knocked on the library door. Normally she would not have been so polite in announcing her entrance, but she knew Father O'Reilly had lately been depressed and this chore of answering the vagrant's questions might give him the purpose he needed. "Father Donovan, Cody is here."

"He is—already?"

"Yes, but Mrs. Wellington is feeding him. She's loaded his plate with enough food to give you another half hour. And she's stoked the fire in your study. So if you were to tell Mrs. Holloway to guide him to that corduroy wingback after he finishes. He'd be asleep in less than ten minutes. You could then sneak in and be sitting at your desk. When he begins to stir, Father Don, you need to be in mid-sentence saying something like, '. . . and that, Cody, is my answer to the last of your questions.'"

"Agnes, you are a clever woman. Is this how you manage Saint Bartholomew's?"

"It might be. Have you seen the exercise I have to go through when the auditor comes in from the archdiocese? Mrs. Holloway and I have worked out our procedure. He ends up sleeping half the time he's here."

"I see. Well, I won't be resorting to such theatrics. Cody asked the questions in good faith and he expects for me to make a similar effort in answering. Show the good man in after he's eaten, please." Father Donovan O'Reilly closed the book he had been reading and stood at his chair.

"You got it, boss."

Fifteen minutes later Agnes knocked, then opened the study door. She turned to Cody standing behind her and said, "Would you care for something to drink?"

"No, ma'am. I'm fine."

"Come in, Cody. Are you warm enough? Have you been working in this inclement weather?" Father O'Reilly reached out his hand.

"Yes, sir. We only got half the trash yesterday. But I'm warming up nicely now." Cody dropped his leather coat and melted into the recesses of the corduroy wingback. "Have you had time to get the answers?"

"I think so. First of all, I can't guarantee that our conference will be completely confidential. If you want our talk to be strictly between you and I, we'll have to go to the confessional." The priest shot a glance to the door. Shadows extended into the room from underneath.

"No, that's quite all right. You're used to working in front of an audience and I appreciate other people thinking my questions are worthy of listening to them being answered."

"Okay. Let me ask you one before we get started. Do you want me to answer with the church's official position or my personal opinion, if it should differ in some small way?"

"I'm only interested in the truth. I assume that, if your opinion differs from the church's, you must think yours is the more accurate. No one would continue to hold an inferior position on purpose."

"Cody, you are a worthy opponent. However, I think we are both looking for the same thing. So let me start by saying the four gospels do differ. Religious historians think Mark was written first, thirty years or so after the death of Jesus. He was followed by Matthew and then Luke, both of which came about forty years after the death of Jesus and included large portions of the earlier work by Mark. Then there was John. He wrote his gospel in approximately AD 95. That's at least twenty years after Matthew and Luke wrote theirs, and sixty years after the crucifixion of our Savior.

"Now, the reason they were written so many years later was that Jesus did not write anything down himself. Nor did he tell his disciples to write anything down. Those early followers were charged with getting the word out and baptizing as many converts as possible. Every follower of Jesus thought the end of the world was imminent. No one took time to write down historical details. Instead, they rushed to evangelize their neighbors to the best of their abilities. Soon they burst through their own localities and took the show on the Roman roads to the gentiles. It wasn't until the people, who had witnessed the events, started dying and new converts clamored for more information that hand-printed treatises started circulating. The people wanted something more reliable than an oral rendition. By the time it was thought the second coming of Jesus might not be an immediate occurrence Stephen, James, Peter, Paul, and others had already died.

"Mark took those oral stories and added what Peter had told him to fashion his Gospel."

"Whoa, Father what makes you think The Gospel of Mark was written by Mark—or any apostle for that matter?"

They heard some guffawing and chair squeaking from just beyond the study door. Father Donovan remained calm. He swallowed, cleared his throat, and continued with, "You are correct. The Gospel of Mark does not say who the author was. In the early days of the church, it was less important to be known as the author of an important book than it was for the book to be read, its lessons learned, and for those lessons to be put into practice. Sometimes a student of a great teacher would use his teacher's name as if to say 'This work is in line with what I have learned from my mentor.' Over the years only the teacher's name would be remembered.

"When the church tried to determine which books belonged to the canon, thereafter, each having the sanction of the Catholic Church, several criteria were considered. If a book was authored by an apostle, it was a shoo-in and bypassed most other tests.

"In the fourth century, a great church historian by the name of Eusebius wrote that Papias, a second-century bishop, said that he prayed for knowledge of the author. He wrote that Mark's name was revealed to Papias by the Holy Spirit in a dream. Papias is also reported to have said that the apostle Matthew wrote the book from then on labeled The Gospel of Matthew. And, while we're on the subject, in AD 180, Irenaeus, a famous Christian writer, identified the apostle John, who lived in Ephesus until the time of Trajan, as the author of The Gospel of John."

"Revealed in a dream?"

"Now, that I do not know. However, the apostles were filled with the Holy Spirit at Pentecost and were enabled to fulfill their mission as charged to them by the resurrected Jesus '. . . to go, therefore, and make disciples of all nations.' The Holy Catholic Church continues what those first apostles started. We believe that we work under the auspices of the Holy Spirit and can trace our authority to Peter. If one of our eminent brothers, who lived a scant eighty years after the fact, says he was inspired by the Holy Spirit to name the author of a book, then who has more authority than he to do so?

"But let's get back to the discrepancies. Each writer wrote for a particular audience. He wasn't writing a history but a treatise designed to reach out to a certain group of people and convince them so thoroughly that they would become believers. Mark, to the Romans needing a short book to the point about a man of action, Matthew, to the Jews who were interested in prophesies being fulfilled, Luke, to the educated and literate gentiles needing information about the humanity of Jesus, and John, to the working-class of gentiles swayed by passion. Half of the entire book of John is about the final week in Jesus' life."

"So, Father, you must be saying that the differences are unimportant. That it's the overall picture that has to be compared. Under that canopy, they are significantly the same."

"Precisely. Each author worked from a cache of oral stories and traditions preserved at different times by different people. Each teller had a different perspective, vocabulary, and opinion as to what he thought important. It amazes me that with the diversity of their treatment they were able to keep so much unity in their subject and make their efforts interesting to the mind while satisfying to the heart."

"Okay. I can accept that answer. What can you tell me about the wandering Jew?"

"How did you hear about that story, Cody?"

"Just in my reading. It cropped up as little interesting asides in several old books."

"Cody, I think you work in a larger arena than I, though I did unearth the details. It seems that in the twelfth century an Armenian archbishop was asked by some monks of St. Albans Abbey about Joseph of Arimathea. They said this Joseph spoke to Jesus and was reported to still be alive.

"The archbishop answered that he himself had seen the man in Armenia and his name was Cartaphilus, a Jewish shoemaker.

"According to the story when Jesus stopped to rest while carrying the cross, this Jew hit Jesus and taunted him to 'Go on quicker, Jesus. Go on quicker. Why dost thou loiter?' Jesus is supposed to have answered in an authoritative voice, 'I shall stand and rest, but thou shall go on till the last day.'

"This old man converted to Christianity and travels the earth proselytizing to those who will listen. He's been sighted in most

European countries under different names and been written about by several different chroniclers."

"That's interesting. Father Don, you should write a novel about him someday. Let's see, that would make him almost two thousand years old. The old man has actually seen and spoken to the Lord. Yes, he might have something to say worth listening to."

Both men turned to the door. They were interested in what their audience was thinking of Father O'Reilly's answers to Cody's questions. There was some noise but nothing to give Father O'Reilly or Cody any indication.

Cody said, "So the last item was Jesus damning the fig tree. What do you have to say about that?"

"Okay, but I would like to have something to drink. All this elucidation has made my throat go dry." From the other side of the door there was some activity. Father O'Reilly waited for a moment before opening it. When he entered the hallway the four chairs were pushed against the wall and their previous occupants had vanished. Father O'Reilly headed to the kitchen and met Mrs. Wellington in the hallway bringing a tray of rattling china teacups and a kettle giving off a curling whiff of steam. "Thank you so much, Mrs. Wellington. Is it going like you had expected?"

"Oh, Father Don, I am so pleased to work for you. Father William and Father Dan have started taking notes. And Agnes. She's gone to retrieve a Bible."

Back in the study, Father Donovan O'Reilly poured steaming tea into two cups and held one out for his guest. "Is this Darjeeling?" asked Cody.

"Yes. Now that the war is over, items that once were rationed have become commonplace." Father Don sat his tea down and leaned back in his chair. He put his hands together and rubbed their palms.

"Now about the fig tree. In Jeremiah 24, God, talking about the dispersion of Israel, compares the Israelites to good and bad figs. He said He would acknowledge those who were carried away captive as the good figs. He said He sent them into the land of the Chaldeans for their own good. The Jews left in Jerusalem He likened to the bad figs. Because of this metaphor Israel was forever prophetically typecast, in a figurative sense, as a fig tree.

"I think, while on the road leaving Bethany, what Jesus said was if Israel did not understand the prophesy concerning his coming and acknowledge and greet him with open arms, they were making a statement about whether they were good figs or bad figs. As this particular tree did not have good figs he, still speaking figuratively, would offer salvation to the gentiles. And allow the fig tree, that is Israel, to wither."

"Please understand, though, that I do not know if this is the view taken by the church. It is only my interpretation."

"I understand. But, it does seem to fit the events." Cody set his right ankle on his knee and said, "Father Don, so far you have answered my questions satisfactorily. But the underlying problem remains. I need proof God exists. It's not sufficient for me to believe that he exists because someone tells me he does. That's the way my parents managed my behavior. When I asked to go to a friend's house and I had not accomplished my chores my mother or father would say 'No' and when I asked why the short answer, their reply was, 'Because I said so.'

"I think the Catholic Church considers its parishioners not astute enough to fathom the depths of religion on their own. They need to be shown the way. As a consequence of this the church answers any questioning for the proof of God by using the pejorative statement 'Because I said so.' And, as their right to answer in such a way, they use a flimsy reference to an attributed saying that itself went through many gyrations before being written down—that is not good enough for me. Does the church have any of the original documents?"

"Not from the Old Testament. We do have early copies from the New Testament writers though."

"Did they think the original documents were not important enough to save?"

"Well, Cody, printing and paper-making were in their infancy. Papyrus came from Egypt, where artisans criss-crossed and glued layers of flattened bullrush. After a few years they crumbled to powder. Parchment was made from the skin of sheep and other animals, and velum was made from the skin of young calves. Neither of these were lasting mediums either. When an author copied a new version, with more illumination, he simply discarded his original. Sometimes he even made changes, thinking his copy was an improvement with better wording or a more accurate translation."

"From what I am hearing, you are telling me the foundation of the church is suspect, the authority by which you govern is puffs of smoke, and the book that guides you is hearsay.

"I want to believe but need something substantial. I want to see how being filled with the Holy Spirit happens and not have to accept that fact without question. I have a hard time accepting the Catholic Church's preeminence. You live in the land of wolves in a house made of chicken fat."

"Cody, that's where faith comes in. You have to have faith the church will not lead you astray. We have almost twenty centuries of experience—."

"Maybe so, but some of that experience was misplaced. Some of that experience was meted out by incompetent, unsavory, unscrupulous malefactors."

"Yes, all institutions of long duration have to re-energize occasionally. The church did that numerous times. After Martin Luther led the way for the Protestant Reformation, the church rekindled its flame and came back more in line with what the original apostles sought. We constantly modify our outreach into the lives of our members and seek new ways to supply what is needed. The church tries to be as modern as it can without changing the tradition or our original charge of taking the good news to all nations."

"Okay, Father, let's call it a day. I'm tired beyond belief."

"Cody, you do look worn out. Are you getting enough sleep?"

"Not lately. I'd like to continue this, but I have to leave while it's still daylight."

"Let me drive you, Cody. We have an old truck we sometimes use. I could put your bike in the . . . Cody." Father O'Reilly was talking to empty space. He walked into the hall and yelled, "Cody, do you need more blankets?"

A hand reached out with a ring of keys. Father Dan said, "Give the man a lift. Have you seen what our weather is doing?"

The wind was blowing too much for Heck to ride his bicycle. It only took a few moments for Father O'Reilly to catch up and very little effort to convince Heck to accept the ride. Except for a few simple directions to the outskirts of town, they rode in silence. Father O'Reilly parked the truck on the road and watched as Heck pushed the bicycle down a slick embankment to his rock and concrete hide-away. Father O'Reilly slapped his thigh as enlightenment set in. He now knew who Cody really was.

CHAPTER 55—AN INTERLUDE BETWEEN SESSIONS
January 1946

The rat lay under one corner of Heck's covers. The day before he ate big holes in a stale loaf of bread and now considered himself a permanent resident. Heck knew some small animal had moved in but was too tired to care. He hardly had time to brush his teeth with a minty twig of cedar before collapsing in a fitful sleep.

As soon as Heck closed his eyes, he slipped into an ongoing dream where his wife appeared. Her clothes ripped, barely escaping the clutches of a madman intent on making her do his bidding. Twists of hair hung down both sides of her face. She lowered her head and kissed Heck on his forehead. "Honey, you did well."

The next morning Heck heard some commotion outside his home. He pulled back a canvas flap for a fellow worker from the Ritz Grand Hotel and Ballroom Bistro. "Gerald, what are you doing here?"

"Hey, Cody. Aren't you going to invite me in? The boss gave me some food and told me not to come back until I had found you. Man, I've been looking for two days. Let me in."

"Okay, but I don't have any chairs—and not much space."

"I won't stay long. Just want to give you this food. Is there anything we can do for you?"

"No, Gerald. I've got a tent heater and St. Bart's gave me all the blankets I could carry."

"The boss said you could move into the kitchen. He's made Pete clean out a closet."

"Thanks anyway, but I have everything I need. That is, except a hot shower."

"You can get one of those any time at my place. Say, did you see that? Something moved by your stack of books. Cody, you've got varmints in here."

"Damn. He better not eat any of those books."

"I'll see you at work. You should eat everything. Don't leave anything for him."

"Thanks, Gerald. Tell Andre I appreciate the food and I'll be back at work in a day or two."

"Mrs. Wellington, tell Father O'Reilly he got a letter from Boston. I think he'll want to open it. His parents live there."

"Thank you, Agnes. I'll tell him as soon as he comes out of the library. He got his locks coiffed at Gena's Beauty Salon earlier this morning and now he's sequestered inside the library with the door locked. Says he doesn't want any distractions. You think Cody will come by? It's been three days."

"I don't know, but I can tell you this. Father Dan and Father William have been talking. They're worried about Father Don. Do you know if he got his hair permed? Both Fathers are glad it's Father Don doing battle with Cody and not one of them. If Cody shows up today we should have a real shooting match. Father Don has been in the library for most of the past three days and we all know how smart that vagrant Cody is."

"Yeah, I think Cody is some big-shot the church sent to test Father Don."

"You might be right. Father Dan and Father William asked me if there's been any communication with the archdiocese during the last few weeks. I'll set this letter on his desk."

"Cody, Paul Mitchell would like to speak with you."

"Who?"

"Tall Paul. You know, that basketball player who plays for the University of Arkansas."

"I still have two loads of dishes to wash."

"Here, dry your hands. They'll still be here when you get back."

"You want me to go into the dining area? I'm not wearing proper clothing."

"Cody, everyone in town knows how hard you work. They know that no one pays you for sweeping their sidewalks. Have you noticed no one throws down litter anymore. They feel bad that you have to pick up after them. You go right on in. The boss said you can take your meal with the customers. Just tell the waiter what you want."

"Okay. Did Tall Paul say what he wanted?"

"No."

Heck didn't want to confront one of his former students, but he couldn't think of a way out. He dried his hands, ran his fingers through his hair, and tucked his shirt inside his pants. After dallying a few more minutes under the scrutiny of the other kitchen workers, Heck went through the swinging kitchen doors to the area with paying customers.

A tall man raised a hand, then stood beside his chair as Heck approached. "Cody, do you have a few minutes? I have some information I think you need to know."

"Mr. Mitchell, they told me I could take my lunch out here. Would you care to join me?"

"It would be my pleasure."

When the waiter came over Paul and Heck ordered from the lunch menu. Heck was adding sugar to his iced tea when Paul said, "What do you think about this weather?"

"It's January. We're supposed to have weather like this."

"I know, but every year it catches me by surprise."

"So, Mr. Mitchell, how do you like college?"

"Mr. Stout—I think we can dispense with the charade between you and I. You know, you are the reason I'm in college. I'm majoring in philosophy. What I've come by to tell you is that the textbook I used in Philosophy 101 was written by you. Did you know that?"

"My book?"

"Yes, sir. They talk about you sometimes. The professors I mean. When I told them you taught me in high school, they were amazed. All except Dean Jacobson. For some reason he doesn't like you one little bit."

"I lived with him for a while, then ran off with his daughter."

"That might do it. He's the department head."

"Was back then, too. He liked my work until he thought his daughter was paying me too much attention. Almost kept me from getting my doctorate, but the other professors spoke up on my behalf and he had to give in. Janet and I eloped hours after I walked across the stage and was given a blank piece of paper wrapped in a purple ribbon."

"I think you should make your peace with him, then come back to the university and teach. It's what you were meant to do."

"I have to find my family before I can do anything. They're being held hostage somewhere while I perform a service."

"Cleaning the city's streets?"

"No. That's a disguise I use while I wheedle through what clues I can find. I've been at it for two years and finally had my first break a few nights ago."

"Mr. Stout, is there anything I can do? No? Well, let me know if you change your mind. Whatever it is, you can count on me."

"I appreciate that, Paul, but this is something I don't want anyone to know about."

"Okay, Mr. Stout, I'll be waiting for you at the Student Union Building. Can I pay for your meal?"

"Don't they let you eat here for free?"

"They've offered, but my coach says we're not allowed to accept."

"Paul, my meal is free. I earn it by washing dishes. But I guess my offering to pay for your meal would fall under that same ethical guideline."

"Yes. We can't accept gifts of any kind from anybody. Andrew has said Santa even marked him off the big list of those naughty and nice."

"I see. Well, thanks Paul for the information. One of these days I need to ask Dean Jacobson where my royalties are. You have a nice trip back and I might see you there one day."

"All right, but I'd like to give you one more bit of advice. In class we talked about why Socrates did not escape when given the opportunity. You said it was because he had given his word to the government. In return for the city-state of Athens providing security for him and his family, educating his children, and providing city services like water and baths and the other niceties of living in one of antiquities' great cities, he was only required to serve in the city's military when it came under attack and to abide by its laws."

"Yes, I remember saying that."

"So when you returned from your sabbatical in the woods, and your family was gone. You thought they had abandoned you because you had embarrassed them in front of their friends. But what really happened was that your narrow-minded landlord evicted them.

"Mr. Stout, just as Socrates had a contract with the state and gave up his life to fulfill that obligation, you have a contract with your wife. You swore to take care of her and to provide for her and to love her. She didn't abandon you. She left because there was no place for her here. You need to find her and fulfill your obligation, just like Socrates did.

"By the way, every one of your students knows what it cost you to tell Mr. Considine you would not betray your personal code of ethics for personal gain. Mr. Stout, you were the one we played that basketball game for when we beat Skunk Hollow. I guess you know that coach Jolly was on their bench with our playbook. We beat him for you."

"No. I didn't know that. I'm proud you thought enough of our friendship to honor me that way. I did see the game. I was one of the fans who jumped up when you went to the free-throw line and screamed 'Throw it like Inez.' Whatever that meant."

"You might like to know Inez is in some of my classes. She and Brad got married and he's working so Inez can finish her degree in clinical psychology. She says they'll be moving back. She wants to offer therapy counseling to the residents of Dancing Deer.

CHAPTER 56—THIRD SESSION
February 1946

Heck was afraid to sleep. He wanted to see his family but didn't want to see them suffer, tormented by an adversary he didn't believe in. Heck had been awake for two days.

Lying under the covers and listening to the wind howl, Heck shivered as the cold had seeped in and overwhelmed his heater. Triangular piles of snow accumulated in the corners and started growing. Then the kerosene ran out. The heater slowly stopped giving heat. The canvas flap covering the opening Heck used as his door popped and snapped from equilibrium changes in pressure. The only one there more upset than Heck was the rat.

Heck pulled the covers over his head. He had to relieve himself, but getting up two hours before daylight and peeing in the snow with your back facing a blizzard was not for weaklings. He lay there and waited for the moment when the need became impossible to ignore. It was not long before Heck sat up, put his shoes on over two layers of socks, and slipped outside. Butt naked, except for five socks and two shoes, Heck shot out a stream thirty feet. He thought, "It must be the wind."

The rat was upset when Heck opened the flap, plummeting the temperature inside down by ten degrees. He shook and scooted under the covers, crawling down to the bottom. Heck finished his business, turned, and shot back in under the flap. He took off his shoes, left on the socks, and climbed in under the covers. Heck slid his feet toward the bottom. He settled in until he felt something move against his foot. The rat thought he was being attacked. He grabbed the hairy intruder with his front paws and snapped down hard with two sharp incisors.

Heck let out a loud scream. He pulled his feet back and, throwing off the covers, jumped out the flap. The rat felt justified and sat up, using a front paw to groom his whiskers. Heck realized he had to get back inside before freezing. He stepped through the flap, skirted the edge of his covers, and fumbled with the matches to get the lantern lit.

Soon Heck sat in one corner wrapped in several blankets. Across the expanse of Heck's quarry abode sat the rat. He and Heck glared at each other. Neither was willing to leave.

Later that morning Heck rode his bicycle to Gerald's house, where he bathed and washed everything he had and was not wearing. Normally, he bathed at one of the two new public bathhouses, but today he went to Gerald's. He hoped he would be offered a bit of breakfast—which would not be available at the public facility. At ten he washed dishes at the Ritz Grand Hotel and Ballroom Bistro. At two he pedaled to Saint Bartholomew's. Father Donovan O'Reilly was waiting.

"Come in, Cody. You look like you could use something warm to drink. Mrs. Wellington, do you have any more of that hot apple cider? Cody, Mrs. Wellington sprinkles nutmeg and cinnamon over a mixture of hard apple cider and melted butter. We call it 'Betsy's Bit of Heaven.' Betsy is Mrs. Wellington's first name."

"You gentlemen go into the study and I'll bring the cider straight away."

Cody removed his leather coat and ragged muffler. He sat in the corduroy wingback and stretched his feet out like he might take a short nap. "Father Don, do you believe in the devil?"

"I do."

"Then you need to know he is the one who sent me to talk with you. It happened in a dream."

"That's one of the ways he communicates."

"So, if the devil exists, then so should God."

"Yes. If one, then the other also."

"What other proof can you offer a hard-headed non-believer?"

"Well, Aristotle thought the form or soul of man is that they have intelligence, or nous, and that they use it to attain God. He thought humans have a deep desire to know and understand truth. In searching for truth, they are participating in God. God is the perfection of understanding. To aspire to God is to aspire to understanding."

"Father, I know a little about Aristotle. He believed that all things strive through a constant process of change to attain the goal that belongs to their own nature. God was regarded by Aristotle as the unmoved mover, from whom all things derive their being and to whom all things, including human beings, strive to return.

"Father, you must have decided that I, being a philosopher of sorts, would be most impressed with the words of one of my most beloved teachers. But I am not interested in what another person thinks—even if he is Aristotle. I am interested in a logical succession of facts that leads to the inescapable conclusion that God does, indeed, exist." Heck poured a cup of Mrs. Wellington's apple cider. He continued, "Do you think Aristotle would have thought the God of the Old Testament was a different God from the one we read about in the New?"

"I don't know. Cody, do you think they might be different gods?"

"A famous philosopher once said that if triangles had a god, their god would have three sides. In the Old Testament it says that God made man in his own image." Heck sipped his steaming beverage. "Boy, Mrs. Wellington should get a copyright on the recipe for this drink." He sat his cup on the edge of an unopened envelope. "I think my philosopher-friend was saying that, man makes his god in his own image. The Jews are a persecuted people, always have been. The only other race of people so ostracized are the gypsies. For the Jews their god would have to be just. Two sayings from the Bible come to mind. Somewhere in Deuteronomy, when Moses was giving the Israelites the punishments for broken laws, as instructed by God, he said '. . . you shall not show pity: life for life, eye for eye, tooth for tooth, hand for hand, foot for foot.'

"Then later in the same book, Moses in his final days gave the Israelites the 'Song of Moses.' I believe it's toward the end of the book. Referring to God he said, 'Vengeance is mine, and retribution.' A few verses later he continued with, 'For the Lord will vindicate his people.' This is the kind of God the Jews wanted. They wanted him to supply them with vengeance, retribution, and vindication against their oppressors.

"In the New Testament Jesus says to love your enemies—to turn the other cheek. So do you think they are the same God?"

"I believe he is the same God, but man's perception of his attributes might have changed."

243

"All right. Do you have any other proofs for me? Something other than 'because I said so?'"

"How about the proof as thought up by Anselm, the Archbishop of Canterbury? He said, 'It is possible to conceive of a being than which nothing greater can be conceived.' And to paraphrase the remainder of his comment he said a being that doesn't exist in the real world would, by definition, be less perfect. So if you can conceive of it and it is greater than the being that does not exist, it must exist."

"Really, Father. That is just a play on words. The philosopher called Zeno once said he could prove that, with a small lead, a tortoise would win a foot-race against Achilles. His proof was that if you believed that Achilles was ten times faster than the tortoise and you started the race by giving the tortoise a ten foot head start. After commencement, if Achilles had sprinted ten feet, he would still be in second place because the tortoise would have traveled one foot. Then when Achilles had traveled that one foot, the tortoise would still be in the lead by a tenth of a foot. This would continue ad infinitum. But it's only a play on words. Have you got anything else?"

"Thomas Aquinas said everything is in a state of motion. Whatever you can imagine, is in motion caused by a prior action. That prior action itself was set into motion by something. This recedes back and further back until you arrive at the foot of the unmoved mover, and that is God."

"Yes. I know about the ontological arguments. But they don't prove anything except there are mysteries difficult to explain. His second proof was that nothing causes itself. Every effect has a prior cause, and this goes back to the first cause which he said was God.

"His third proof was there must have been a time when no physical things existed. But, since physical things exist now, there must have been something non-physical to bring them into existence, and that something non-physical was God." Cody took another sip.

"You're shooting me out of the water, Cody. How about we add a little Aristotle to Thomas Aquinas. Consider that everything in nature strives to achieve it's natural state and that state of being is perfection for the item in question. Now, man is both good and bad. The maximum goodness or perfection man strives for cannot reside in himself.

Therefore there must be some other maximum to set the standard for perfection. That standard is God."

"Yeah, some men smell worse than others. If man tries to achieve the maximum conceivable stink, there must exist an unmatchable stinkeroo and that Pooh Bah of stench is God."

"Cody, I've got one more, then I am out of proofs. This is called the argument from design. Before you build something, it must be designed. Take a fine watch for example. When I was sixteen my father gave me his father's pocket watch. I used to raise it's lid and listen to it chime the hours. Then one day I got the bright idea that I wanted to see how the thing worked. When my dad got home that evening, I had the watch in a million pieces. He didn't give me a spanking or anything like that, but I could see he was disappointed in me. That hurt more than a whipping. And what I gathered from my experience was that the watchmaker was gifted in the intricacies of tiny gears, springs, and levers. He was the master of small things in tight spaces.

"How much more delicately designed is the photosynthesis process. How much more minute is the living cell. And these all had to be designed by something or somebody. To my thinking, it was the world's best watchmaker to the nth degree, who could only be God."

"To that, I say you need to read Charles Darwin's *The Origin of Species*."

Father O'Reilly got up from his chair and filled another glass of Betsy's Bit of Heaven. He walked to the window and looked out over the stillness of a white landscape un-defiled in its serene beauty. He shuddered at the thought of people like Cody living with little protection against the harsh reality of an unforgiving universe. He had one last card to play.

"Cody, say you are a betting man. You have to bet your life on the existence or non-existence of God. If you take the side that God exists and live your life accordingly and you're right, you will have won eternal bliss. You will dwell in the presence of the Deity. You will have your wife and family at your side. However, if you bet that way and you're wrong what have you lost? Nothing. True, some details you would have to endure: baptism, the Eucharist, confession, and a few others. But nothing you would object to. Your high ethical standards mean you are already living a comparatively sin-free existence. So you have everything to gain and hardly anything to lose.

"Now, let's suppose you choose the other side. You don't believe in God. If you're correct, when you die nothing happens. But suppose you're wrong. Your wife and children are in heaven. And you, damned in hell, will live through eternity out of their presence and in continued torment.

"So, Cody, being the logical person you are, tell me which position has everything to gain and nothing to lose? And which position has nothing to gain and everything to lose? Which is your choice?"

Cody held his bowed head in his hands. He ran his fingers through his hair. "But my wife."

"She's in Fayetteville."

"What?"

"I went to the beauty shop this morning. Gena knows everything that goes on in this town. She said your wife came in the day before she left and got her hair styled."

Cody leaped out of his chair, grabbed his coat, and ran out the door. He had to jump over Mrs. Wellington's lap in the hallway, as she was slower than the others in getting out of his way.

Father O'Reilly took a big breath of air and sat down at his desk before letting it all out. He started stacking the notes he'd prepared. He thought he might write a book someday about the test of faith he had endured at the hands of a formidable philosopher. Then he saw it. A letter with his name written by a shaky hand. The postmark was Boston.

Father Donovan O'Reilly ripped it open and pulled out a single sheet of folded paper. It gave an address and a single sentence written in large letters. It read, "*Help me, Ivanhoe.*"

The End

Author Bio

Ron Lambert, an examined life

As an accountant in a small West Texas town, I spend my days studying the bank statements and tax returns of other people's businesses. I classify, summarize, and display their financial transactions in some meaningful format. I love creating order out of chaos.

I'm middle-aged and twice married—with the second blessed from heaven. Four grown children, their children, two bobbing tails of barking energy, and one sly cat round out my cache of treasure.

Over the years I have owned two retail stores, several service businesses, one ranch, and one restaurant. I have been prosperous and poor, with wild fluctuations in between. At present, being neither rich nor poor, I consider my status as deeply entrenched in middle class—a term bandied about by politicians and economists.

In an effort to restore my youth I purchased an old sofa on two wheels. For the past ten years, I have occasionally strapped sacks of clothes, maps, and a compass that doesn't seem to work onto the back cushion. After kissing my wife I set out for adventure and story. Usually, after only a week or so, I realize what I left behind was more important than what I set out to find and drive a day and a night hell-bent-for-leather back home.

I then settle into an old and comfortable routine. I read a few books, attend a few plays, daydream of new horizons, and plan my next adventure. I kept a journal on my first excursion. It was such an exhilarating experience: rewriting the journal and incorporating the pictures I took, that I became intoxicated to the point I wrote a novel.

At present, with pen on fire, I'm scratching out the ending for my seventh book. I'll win prestigious awards and be asked to speak at the local library if someone would read what I have written.

If you're looking for an evening spent with colorful and mesmerizing characters, if you want to immerse yourself in a rollicking good story, enthrall yourself to the point of madness, go two days without bathing, then have I got a story for you.

Additional Novels
Continuing the Dancing Deer Story

Soon all will be available in multiple formats at Amazon.com. Trade Paperbacks in perfect binding can be purchased at our corporate office and from display stands in several of our fine businesses in Columbus, Texas

Dancing Deer (Book 1)

Dancing Deer is the embodiment of small-town America. When asked, she sent her sons to war. This is the story of The Calhoun—one of those boys. It's also about his fellow combatants, the men he served, the men he fought, and the women who loved him.

There is the French Resistance, the German Gestapo, *Midge at the Mike*, Anzio Annie, the *Gustav Line*, and the US Army's Forty-Fifth Infantry Division campaigning from Sicily through Italy and France pushing back the formidable Germans. But this story is so much more.

Find a comfortable chair and settle in with a great new book. You won't be disappointed.

The Last Dance (Book 2)

Bill Potter is charged with murdering his Friday night squeeze. His bumbling lawyer steps out of a dead-end job of contracts and leases to save Bill from being strapped to "Old Spanky." Bill's wife returns after a twenty year absence to muddy the waters and it's up to her and Pepe, the womanizing Resistance fighter and WWI spy from France, to solve the case.

The Measure of a Man (Book 3)

A group of Cuban immigrants decide to barnstorm the Midwest, entertaining the towns they come to with a game of ball. When they get to Dancing Deer the men on the city council con Bill Potter into a wager for more than they can afford to lose. Bill's position is that the Men from Dancing Deer will prevail. With a team of misfits and one win under their belts Bill goes in search of a new manager. His ex-wife is traveling throughout the Western US with Pepe, the French womanizer. She knows more about ball than anyone and he has to convince her to come back and once again save him from the wolves at the door.

Lost in Appalachia (Book 4)

Dancing Deer's Chief of Police is lost in the mountains of West Virginia. Suffering from an injury, he can't remember who he is or why he's lost. Two kids take him in and hide him from a determined fiancée. She offers a big reward and the chief thinks he must have committed a major crime for someone to pony up such a large bounty.

Christmas in Dancing Deer (Book 5)

St. Bartholomew's is consolidating its orphanage, but the children don't want to be separated. They come up with an alternative plan to present to the church but then the women of Dancing Deer bring the orphan girls into their homes for the holidays. The boys leave on their own, in the snow, and spend a night with a burdened bank robber in a desolated cabin.

Beggarman, Thief (Book 6)

A story of a bank robber who finds his moment of epiphany in a shack with six lost little boys. He goes home after twenty years on the lamb to have Christmas with his family and to right his wrongs. But he finds his past is in hot pursuit and the new life he has found is in jeopardy. He runs away in the clutches of a pretty lady evangelist who is taking her show on the road to the very town where he committed his last crime.

Toe to Toe with A Drunken Philosopher

This is really one story in three parts. First we have the high school philosophy teacher who has to resign his position much as Aristotle had to when the authorities in Athens came looking for him. Part number two is of an indigent Irish family who emigrate from the Emerald Isle. The little Irish boy in the family grows up to become a priest. Then the third part pits the philosopher and the priest in a contest of wits.

Racing the Wind   (Book 7, but not yet finished)

A story of a boy with plans to someday build bridges or design skyscrapers. He decides to start with a racer in the Soapbox Derby. Problems, orchestrated by his main adversary, creep into the racer's production. The boy has to rely on the help of a fellow classmate—a girl—to find the source of his problem and to finish the racer and the race.

Order Form

Book Name	Qty	Price	Extension
Dancing Deer	☐	$17.95	_____
The Last Dance	☐	$15.95	_____
The Measure of a Man	☐	$15.95	_____
Lost in Appalachia	☐	$15.95	_____
Christmas in Dancing Deer	☐	$15.95	_____
Beggarman, Thief	☐	$15.95	_____
Toe to Toe with a Drunken Philosopher	☐	$15.95	_____

Sub-Total _____

Sales Tax (for Texas purchases) @8.25%   _____
Shipping: $4.00 for 1st Book
          $2.00 for each Additional   _____

Grand Total _____

Would you like your book(s) autographed? Yes ☐ **No** ☐

Would you like your book(s) wrapped?   Yes ☐ ☐

To_____ From_____

Order Form (continued)

Name _____

Shipping Address:
Military APO _____

Street or PO Box _____

State and Zip _____

Telephone _____

Payment:
Check Enclosed [ ]

Credit Card:
Discover [ ]

Visa [ ]

MasterCard [ ]

Card Number _____

Expiration Date _____

Code (on back) _____

Keep Credit Card Information for future purchases [ ]

Order Form (instructions)

Boxes   Place quantity or checkmark (X) where applicable

Mail Completed Form To:
> Printers Guild Publishing, llc
> 425 Spring Street, Suite 101
> Columbus, Texas 78934-2461

Or Fax Form to:
> (979) 733-0015

Or Call-In Your Order:
> (979) 732-2962

For Pick-Up:
> You are welcome to come by our office in the Stafford Opera House at 425 Spring Street, Suite 101, Columbus, Texas to pick up your order and save shipping costs or to talk with the author.
> Please call (979) 732-2962 to make sure someone will be there.

Security
> We do not share any of your information with anyone. We do not keep your credit card information unless you check the box allowing us to do so for future purchases.